S

Dune House Cozy Mystery Series

Cindy Bell

Copyright © 2014 Cindy Bell

All rights reserved.

ISBN-13: 978-1500172329

ISBN-10: 1500172324

Table of Contents

Chapter One

At first glance the intricate architecture of the roof that rose against the early morning gray sky would take anyone's breath away. The wide eyes of its large attic windows seemed to stare down at the town it resided in, with a subtle affection. The grand, old building was very well known in the small seaside town of Garber. It was the toast of the town in the past, as it was the largest and oldest structure, and had traditionally served as the home of the wealthiest family in town. Over the years, it had changed as much as the town surrounding it had. Garber was a tiny town of only just over two thousand people. Its main businesses were tourist traps and the minimum required to keep a town functioning. It ran the length of a secluded beach, with a bustling town square as its social center.

At one time the quaint environment had drawn the wealthiest of the wealthy, but things had changed since then. Because it was a good distance from anything modern or convenient it had become a less popular destination. The younger crowds wanted to be near nightclubs and the most fashionable stores and restaurants. The older crowds preferred vacationing somewhere more exotic that boasted other amenities, like spas and all-inclusive resorts. Garber fell out of fashion, and seemed to fall out of the progression of time, too. Its buildings began to fade and become run down. Developers were interested in purchasing the properties because it was close to the beach, but the older residents of the town fought against it. They didn't want their town to be bulldozed and turned into a resort or a theme park. Their children moved away to find work, as there was little employment in the town.

The grand, old home that used to be the center of the town, affectionately referred to as Dune House because of its proximity to the beach, became the prime example of the towns steady downfall. Dune House had been converted into a bed and breakfast by its most recent owners, Beverly and Harry Allen, but it was closed to the public after Beverly passed away. Harry Allen spent the rest of his days as a recluse inside the walls of the home and showed little interest in its upkeep. After his recent death, the town breathed a collective sigh as if this was yet another sign of the town fading away.

Garber had a mayor who decided it was time for their town to have a new outlook. He began rallying to have developers come into the town and take over what properties they could. He began marketing Dune House as an excellent piece of property for the developers. However, before he could offer it up, he had to get in contact with the relative that Harry Allen had willed the property to, a niece who had not seen him in decades, Suzie Allen.

Suzie lived a pretty laid back lifestyle. She had a small condo that she enjoyed decorating. She filled her time with reading novels, and spending fun days out with her best friend, Mary Brent. Suzie had been friends with Mary since they were in high school together. They had remained friends, even when Mary's life grew very busy with marriage and two children to raise. Suzie had no interest in marriage or children, she found satisfaction in working as an investigative journalist for a regional newspaper. She was always investigating something, and coming up with new ideas for stories for the papers to run. However, since the digital age had struck Suzie found journalism to be less about the story and more about marketing. She decided to bow out of the field and pursue her creative side.

Suzie had dabbled in interior decorating, and adored looking into the history of old buildings and how they had changed through the years. She dreamed of restoring an old building. However, in a town as fast-paced and modern as Burlington, she knew there was little chance of that. Not to mention the cost. Her career as a journalist had left her with a comfortable retirement but nothing that could finance purchasing a historical building.

Now in her fifties, Suzie was feeling a little more restless. She had lived in the same place for so long that she sometimes forgot there was an entire world outside the city limits. She was finishing the latest suspense novel she was reading when the ring of her cell phone startled her. She eyed it with animosity. She was at a very good part in her book and considered not answering it at all. But the ring was persistent. She snatched it up and was happy to see that it was her friend, Mary, calling.

"Hi, gorgeous!" Suzie greeted Mary cheerfully as she answered the phone.

"Oh, Suzie," Mary gasped into the phone, and Suzie knew right away that this was not going to be a happy call.

"What's wrong, Mary?" Suzie asked quickly. "Is it the kids?" She knew that Mary's children, a boy Benjamin, and a girl Catherine, were away at college. She had stood with Mary the day she had to say goodbye to each of them. Mary's whole life had been built around her children. She had been a housewife since Benjamin was born, and though she was very proud of both of her children starting their own lives, it had been heartbreaking for her, too. Not to mention that she was left to face alone the horrid man she called a husband. Suzie was not a fan of Kent, and she had let Mary know that from day one. But Mary had been in love, and Kent hadn't shown his true colors until after they were married.

"It's Kent," Mary admitted with a sigh and a sniffle. "I can't believe he's doing this, but he's taking the house, the car, everything."

"Oh, Mary, I'm sorry," Suzie said gently. She would never tell her friend, 'I told you so'. Mary had been through so much with her husband, and Suzie knew that she regretted trusting him. But his name was on everything they owned. "Why don't you come stay with me?" Suzie suggested. "Get away from him for a while, we'll get you a good lawyer and we'll fight for the house..."

"No," Mary said with determination, and a strength in her voice that Suzie hadn't heard in a long time. "I don't even want the house, Suzie. I don't want the car, I don't want anything that reminds me of him. The kids are okay now, they have their own lives, and it's way past time for me to start my own. I'm not going to let him take one more day from me."

"I'm proud of you, Mary," Suzie said quickly. "It's time for you to think about you a little."

"Thank you, Suzie," Mary sighed and Suzie

could hear the hurt in her friend's voice. It broke Suzie's heart to think of her suffering, but it also made her feel excited that Mary would finally have some freedom from a man who had done his best to keep her under lock and key.

"Come over, I've got a bottle of wine with your name on it," Suzie smiled into the phone, she knew that Mary wouldn't be able to resist.

"I'll be there in ten," Mary replied before hanging up the phone.

Suzie didn't have a lot of family in her life and she felt very lucky to have Mary. She busied herself getting the wine and wine glasses ready, and completely forgot about the last chapter of her book. When the phone rang again, Suzie picked it up quickly, thinking it was Mary.

"Hey, beautiful," she said, anticipating that it was Mary.

"Uh, is this Suzie Allen?" an unfamiliar voice asked with a slight stammer.

Suzie winced as she realized she must have accidentally answered a sales call.

"May I ask who's calling?" she countered

without admitting her identity.

"This is Bill Cooper, I'm an estate lawyer for your uncle, Harry Allen," he explained quickly.

"Uncle Harry?" Suzie asked with surprise as she sat down on the edge of her couch. She hadn't thought of her uncle in many years. "Has he passed?" she asked with concern.

"I'm sorry, but yes," Bill replied with a waver in his voice. "I've been trying to contact you for over a week. I'm afraid he passed almost two weeks ago, from a sudden heart attack."

"Oh my," Suzie sighed as she closed her eyes briefly. "I'm sorry, I haven't seen him in so long. I guess I missed the funeral?"

"Yes, again, I'm sorry for your loss," Bill said in a professional tone. "But I'm calling to inform you that Mr. Allen named you in his will."

"Me?" Suzie shook her head. "There must be some mistake. I haven't seen him since I was a child."

"No mistake," Bill said firmly. "He's left you his property in Garber."

Suzie was silent for a long moment as she

attempted to recall the house he was referring to. "Dune House?" he prompted.

"Dune House," Suzie said with a wide smile as the memories flooded her. She had called it a castle as a child. "But, doesn't he have any children?" Suzie asked with confusion. "And what about Aunt Beverly?"

"I'm sorry to tell you Suzie, but Beverly Allen died a few years ago. Harry does have a son, Jason, but he did not leave the property to him, he left it to you," Bill said firmly.

Suzie was stunned by his words. She hadn't thought of Beverly or Harry for a very long time. Harry was her father's younger brother, and they had had a strained relationship. She had heard briefly about a child being born when she was in her teens, but she had never been told about Beverly's passing.

"Well, this is very surprising," Suzie said quietly as she tried to process the idea of inheriting such a large property.

"I'll need you to come to Garber to sign some papers," the lawyer said. "He left you the property, the home, and all of its contents. Will you be able to travel to Garber?"

Suzie hesitated for a moment. She really had no reason not to go. In fact, she had been hoping for something to shake her life up a bit. It might also be nice to meet her cousin and find out what he was like.

"Sure, I can be there this week," she offered as a bit of excitement began to build within her. She felt a little guilty for being thrilled considering that her uncle had passed, but she could barely recall his face, let alone anything personal about him. The house she had stared up at as she had built sandcastles on the beach however, she could remember very clearly.

***

When Mary arrived at Suzie's condo, Suzie's mind was still spinning with the news of the inheritance, and the loss of her uncle. After her father had died when she was just a teenager, she hadn't kept in contact with his side of the family, considering that he hadn't seemed too interested in keeping in contact with them either. Now, the phone call had stirred up a lot of curiosity in Suzie. She opened the door for Mary with a dazed look in her eyes.

Mary stepped inside with her suitcase and smiled at Suzie. "Are you okay?" she asked when she noticed the distant expression on her face.

"I think so," Suzie nodded and swept her shoulder length hair back over her shoulders. Since she had started to spot some grays in her forties she had been dying it a brassy gold color that seemed to suit her tanned skin and her bright blue eyes. She felt it was important to maintain a youthful appearance since society seemed to demand it. Mary on the other hand had left her looks up to nature. She had gray streaks running through her auburn hair, which Suzie actually thought made the loose curls of her mid-back length hair even more luxurious. Her deep brown eyes were soulful, and seemed to be holding more sorrow lately than they should have been.

"I'm fine, but what about you?" Suzie asked and hugged her best friend close. In truth, they were more like sisters than friends.

"I will be fine," Mary promised her. They spent the entire night sitting up discussing the past, Mary's children, Suzie's career, and the ending of Mary's marriage. At some point Suzie brought up the property she had inherited.

"What a surprise," Mary smiled at the news. "Are you looking forward to checking it out?"

"Oh, I'll probably just sign whatever papers I need to in order to sell it," Suzie shrugged dismissively.

"But Suzie, this is what you've always dreamed of," Mary reminded her with a frown. "Are you sure you want to sell it?"

"From what he said it needs a lot of work," Suzie sighed as she thought of the beautiful house she remembered becoming run down, but that was how Bill had described it. "I'm not sure I'm up to doing it all by myself."

"You should at least go and see it," Mary insisted. "Maybe it's not as run down as he's saying."

"Maybe," Suzie frowned. "I feel badly that I missed my uncle's funeral. Apparently, he passed away almost two weeks ago. I didn't even know."

"I'm sorry, Suzie," Mary murmured sympathetically.

"I know I barely knew him, but I wish I had thought to reconnect with him," Suzie admitted as she sat back against the couch. "I guess time just gets away from us."

"It sure does," Mary sighed as she took a sip of her wine. "I never thought I'd be in my fifties starting my life over again," she laughed with a mixture of giddiness and fear.

Suzie laughed with her and they clinked their wine glasses together in a toast to Mary's new life. Then Mary trailed her fingertip thoughtfully along the rim of her glass.

"So, don't let another moment pass you by, Suzie," she encouraged her friend. "This is a chance of a lifetime. Go to Garber and get to know the house that your uncle lived in, you might be able to get to know a little about him, too."

"Maybe I will," Suzie nodded a little and then met Mary's eyes. "But only if you come with me."

"Me?" Mary laughed a little. "I don't know if I could do that."

"Why not?" Suzie pushed as her blue eyes began to shine with renewed excitement. "Like you said, you want to get away."

Mary thought about it for a moment and then nodded slowly. "You know, you're right," a slow smile spread across her lips. "Let's do it," she said, her smile becoming a wide grin. "It'll be so much fun!"

"Yes it will," Suzie agreed and they clinked their glasses one more time.

Chapter Two

The next few days were a whirlwind of packing and getting things in place so that Suzie could be away for an indeterminate amount of time. More than anything she was thrilled to have the time to spend with Mary, and to get her away from the pain that Kent was insisting on inflicting on her. He called several times just to give Mary updates about the legal steps he was taking. Mary ignored the calls at Suzie's insistence. By the time they set out on their five hour drive to Garber, Mary was smiling more and seemed to be looking forward to the journey.

"When was the last time we took a trip together, just you and I?" Suzie asked with a fond smile as they drove down the highway.

"I think it was that cruise," Mary cringed as she recalled the disaster of a 'girls' vacation they had taken. First there had been the fight to even get Kent to agree to it, then there was the inclement weather that left Mary holed up in the bathroom because of seasickness.

"Ah, yes," Suzie chuckled. "The cruise that

shall not be spoken of," she grinned around the name they had given it many years ago.

"At least this one will be on dry land," Mary pointed out with relief in her voice.

"That's true," Suzie laughed as she turned off on the exit that would lead them to Garber.

"So, you've never met your cousin?" Mary asked as she gazed out the window. "How old is he?"

"In his thirties, I think," Suzie shook her head. "It's strange to think that I have a relative that I've never even laid eyes on. From what the lawyer told me, he's a police officer."

"Oh dear," Mary frowned as she raised an eyebrow in Suzie's direction. "I can remember the last time you were in handcuffs."

"That was a simple misunderstanding," Suzie insisted with an innocent smile.

"Mmhm, it was a misunderstanding that got you a night in jail," Mary reminded her with a soft laugh. "I can remember that phone call in the middle of the night. When I woke up, I thought uh oh one of the kids is in trouble, imagine my surprise when I heard your voice on the other end of the line."

"It was for a story," Suzie giggled at the memory. The truth was she had been terrified at the time. She had let her role as an investigative reporter get a little out of control by impersonating a police officer, which apparently other police officers did not take kindly to. In the end she had been released because of her spotless record, but it had been a scary night of staring at the stark white ceiling of her cell and wondering if she was going to have to go before a judge. It had made her far more cautious about the risks she was willing to take to get a story, and what stories she was interested in investigating. After that she stuck to less dangerous stories, keeping her focus on politics and consumer issues.

"Let's make the most of this," Mary said softly as she continued to gaze through the window. "I'm ready to see what life has in store for both of us."

"Me too, Mary," Suzie smiled to herself.

***

When they arrived in Garber it was early afternoon. The air was laced with the scent of salt, and a hint of rain hanging in the air. Suzie stepped out of the car and breathed in deeply. It made her entire body relax. She had always loved the beach, and had spent many summer days with Mary and her children exploring whatever beach they were close enough to reach. She had always found the sea and the mysteries it held to be enchanting. That was why she had talked Mary into the terrible cruise trip they had taken. Though Mary had sworn never to set foot on a boat again, Suzie actually missed being out on the open water. It had been very freeing to feel as if she was detached from dry land. Until of course, the storm had hit.

"Wow," Mary breathed out as she stared up at Dune House surrounded by the deep blue sky of the afternoon. "You weren't kidding about this place."

"I know," Suzie sighed as she turned to face it. "It needs a lot of work," she murmured as she looked from the dangling shutters to the sagging porch.

"No, that's not what I meant," Mary said quickly as she continued to stare at the building. "I meant it's as beautiful as you described it."

"You've been here before?" a voice asked from behind both of them, causing Suzie to jump slightly and Mary to squint against the bright sun.

A man in a police uniform was standing before them. He even wore a hat, and a gun in a holster at his side. Suzie felt vaguely nervous when she spotted the handcuffs on his utility belt.

"Once, when I was a child," Suzie replied as she studied him intently. "You must be Jason."

"I am," he replied in a clipped tone. His expression was calm, but his gaze was searching her curiously.

"I'm sorry that I missed the funeral, Jason," she said softly as she studied the young man. He was in his thirties and quite handsome in his uniform. Suzie could tell that he resembled her father a little around his bold blue eyes, and in

19

the curve of his thin lips. He had that same calm and logical gaze that her father had often worn. She imagined that her uncle must have had the same expression, but she didn't recall it. The only thing unexpected about him was the thick, red hair that peeked out from beneath his hat, which Suzie recalled was the same shade as her Aunt Beverly's. He looked a little uncomfortable as he stood before her, and adjusted the gun in the holster on his hip.

"It's all right," he shrugged and then hesitated a moment. "I don't think I ever met you," he said quietly. "I'm sorry I can't recall if I did."

"No, you didn't," Suzie replied with a warm smile. "I lost contact with your father and his family after my father died."

"Oh," Jason nodded and glanced away, still quite nervous. "I'm sorry for your loss."

"Thank you, and I'm sorry for yours," she murmured in return. "Losing a parent is never easy."

"No," Jason agreed, his eyes cold as they looked back at her. "It isn't, I'm just here to give you this," he explained as he handed her a small envelope. "I had some of the keys to the house, and also there's some paperwork in there from Bill Cooper. He can't meet you this afternoon, but said he would be happy to meet you tomorrow."

"Thank you," Suzie replied as she took the envelope from him. "It's good to meet you, Jason," she said with a smile.

"You too, Suzie," he replied with a nod of his head.

"Oh, I'm sorry," Suzie laughed, feeling a little flustered. "This is my friend Mary," she pulled Mary over beside her. "She's going to be staying here with me while we get everything straightened out."

"Nice to meet you, Mary," Jason nodded curtly. Mary nodded and smiled in return.

"I'll let you two get to it," he said with a shrug and then started to turn away. He glanced back over his shoulder as if he had just remembered something. "The place, it needs a lot of work. I know there is an offer on the table, a very generous one," he met Suzie's eyes. "It would be best if you settled things quickly."

"Oh," Suzie nodded, a little taken back by his bluntness. He nodded again and then walked off to his patrol car. Suzie glanced over at Mary. "What was that about?" she asked with widened eyes.

"Who knows," Mary shrugged as she and Suzie began walking up to Dune House. "One thing about long lost family, Suzie, there are always things you would prefer not to find out."

"That might just be the case," Suzie agreed as the patrol car tore off down the driveway.

***

When they made it inside of what was most recently a B & B, Mary and Suzie were both startled by the state of it. Although the outside was certainly untended, there was some expectation that the inside would be a little better. Instead they found layers of dust, furniture covered in sheets, and a kitchen that looked as if it hadn't been used for anything but the microwave and the trash can for years. There wasn't a dish in the sink, but there was still a trash can piled with paper plates, old dinner packages, and boxes from local take out places.

"Hmm, looks like he didn't leave home too much," Mary said when she opened the fridge and found it nearly bare, aside from a six-pack of beer, with two bottles missing. "Was he a drinker?"

"Honestly, I don't know," Suzie shook her head as she glanced around. "I was thinking perhaps we could salvage it, but..."

"But what?" Mary asked as she wiped her finger through a layer of dust on the refrigerator door. "Nothing a little elbow grease won't cure," she smiled.

"Seriously?" Suzie scrunched up her nose. "I can only imagine that the rest of the place is just as bad."

"Don't think of it as a whole, we'll just take it room by room," Mary insisted and then reached down to pick up some trash from the floor. "Trust me, I've seen worse disasters than this."

"Well, if you're game I am, too," Suzie said

with renewed confidence. They worked on the kitchen for a few hours, and then moved into the living room. When it began to grow dark they decided to call it a day. Since there was currently no power to the house they retired to the motel room that Suzie had booked for them. The motel was on the outskirts of town, and there were only a few other cars in the parking lot. It was quaint, clean, and most importantly had comfortable mattresses. They were both worn out from the day and eager to get some good sleep, but the moment they lay down, they also realized they were starving.

"I think I spotted a vending machine in the hall," Suzie said as Mary sprawled out on her bed. "I'll go grab us something to munch on."

"Sounds perfect," Mary agreed with a smile.

As Suzie walked out into the open air hallway that led to both the ice machine and the vending machine she noticed how quiet her surroundings were. She hadn't heard such comforting silence in a very long time. Though the motel was not on the water, she could hear the distant crashing of the waves. She was so distracted by the peacefulness of her environment that she didn't notice a discarded ice bucket in her path until she struck it with her foot which became entangled in the handle.

"Oops," she gasped out as she fell forward and braced herself to strike the cold concrete. Instead she landed against the firm chest of someone who caught her in mid-fall.

"Careful there," he murmured in a deep, smooth voice.

"Oh, thank you," Suzie said as she straightened up quickly and brushed back a few strands of her hair. She smiled as she looked up into the man's cool gray eyes. They gazed out at her from beneath bushy, brown eyebrows, set on top of a face weathered by sun and wind. He looked to be in his fifties, and though his dark brown hair was thick it only covered a portion of his scalp.

"Are you all right?" he asked with concern, his hand lingering on her elbow as she pried the bucket off her foot.

"I'm fine," she promised and blushed at the same time. "A little embarrassed, but fine."

"You're not from around here, are you?" he

asked as he took the bucket from her and set it beside the ice machine.

"Is it that obvious?" she asked with a sheepish smile.

"No, it's just that I know every beautiful woman in town, and," he paused a moment as he looked back at her, "I've never met you before."

"Aw, quite the charmer," she smiled at him and shook her head. "My uncle, Harry Allen, was from here," she explained.

"Oh, Harry was your uncle?" he asked with surprise. "He was a good man," he said in a softer tone. "I'm sorry for your loss."

"I appreciate your sympathy," Suzie replied as he finally released her elbow. "I didn't have the chance to know him well. Were you friends?"

"Not exactly," he replied and ran a hand along the grizzled slope of his chin. "Harry wasn't really friends with anyone after Beverly died. He kept to himself mostly. But he was always willing to give a helping hand to those in need. At least, before he holed himself up in Dune House."

"He left Dune House to me," Suzie said with a slight frown. "I still don't understand why."

"Oh, I can tell you why," he said with a nod of his head. "It's to keep it out of the hands of his boy, and that greedy fool we call a mayor."

Suzie raised her eyebrows with surprise. "Why would he want to keep it away from Jason?"

"He wouldn't, I'd guess," the man shrugged and shoved his hands into his pockets. "It's just that Jason has become very close to the mayor, and the mayor wants that property. I'm sure if Jason had inherited it, he would have handed it right over. It's a shame what happened to Harry. He was healthy as a horse the last time I saw him. It's hard to imagine that his heart just gave out."

"It is sad," Suzie agreed in a wistful tone. "I wish I had known him when I had the chance."

"I'm Paul by the way," he said as he offered her his hand.

"Suzie, Suzie Allen," Suzie replied and shook his hand. "It's nice to meet you, Paul, and thank you for your help."

"No trouble at all. If you need anything, I'm staying in room eighteen for a few days. I have a boat on the water, but since the waves have been rough the past few days I'm treating myself to some solid ground," he smiled a little at that.

"Thanks again," Suzie said with a nod as she walked over to the vending machine. As he walked away, Suzie watched him retreat through the reflection in the glass in the front of the machine. His words about her uncle made her wonder if that might really have been the reason why Harry had left the house to her. Maybe he was hoping that she would see more value in it than his son did. When she returned to the room with snacks, she found Mary already snoring in her bed. Suzie smiled and covered her up, before settling into her own bed. Despite how tired she was she found it difficult to sleep. Her mind was filled with thoughts of Dune House, of Jason, and of her Uncle Harry.

Chapter Three

The next morning Mary and Suzie woke early to head back to work on the house. On the way to the house they decided to stop off at the local diner to have some coffee and breakfast. When they walked in, the locals looked up at them curiously. Suzie offered a friendly smile as Mary selected a table. They were barely seated when a waitress walked up to them.

"What can I get for you?" she asked in a friendly tone.

"We'll start with some coffee," Mary smiled in return.

"I'm going to use the restroom," Suzie said as she stood up from the table. Mary nodded and began perusing the breakfast menu. When Suzie returned from the restroom she nearly walked right into Jason, who was waiting for her.

"Oh sorry," he said when she gasped. "I didn't mean to startle you."

"It's fine," she said quickly. "I just wasn't expecting anyone to be standing here."

"I saw your car, and wanted to speak with you," he explained and stepped a little closer to her. "I just want to remind you that if you need help with anything, you're welcome to call me any time."

Mary was watching from the table they had been seated at. She sipped her coffee as she studied the interaction between the two.

"Jason, do you mind if I ask you a question?" Suzie asked gently.

"Sure," Jason shrugged and locked eyes with her. She could tell that he likely excelled in his role as a police officer as she had barely seen him blink the entire time they'd been talking. He seemed like a very serious, young man, perhaps with something he thought he needed to prove.

"Why did the lawyers call me?" Suzie asked as she looked openly back at him. "Why would your father leave the bed and breakfast to me and not to his son?"

"Ah," Jason nodded slowly. "I guess you really were out of touch. My father and I had a falling out after my mother passed," he admitted and cleared his throat.

"I'm sorry, I didn't mean to pry," Suzie murmured, though that was exactly what she had meant to do.

"It's okay," Jason shrugged again as if nothing could disturb him. "My father and I never really saw eye to eye. To be honest, not leaving the house to me was probably the only gesture of kindness he ever offered me. I wouldn't live in that place if someone paid me to," he paused a moment and glanced over his shoulder before looking back at her. "To be honest, Suzie, you're getting the short end of the stick. My father did leave me an inheritance, what he left you is a rotting pile of junk, and it might cost you more to get it liveable than it's worth."

"Oh?" Suzie asked, thinking that Jason's opinion confirmed what Paul had said the night before. She was glad that Jason hadn't been left completely out of the will, but she wondered why he had such bad memories about the home itself. "I hadn't planned on just getting rid of it," she added. "Mary and I are going to refurbish it, once it's fixed up we might decide to sell it. I'd be happy to split the profits with you," she added in a light tone.

"That's very kind of you," Jason pursed his lips slightly. "But honestly, I'd rather see the place bulldozed. I'm sure there are a few offers on the table since the property is right on the beach. From what I understand the mayor is even interested."

"I'm sorry to disappoint you," Suzie replied in a firmer tone after he mentioned the mayor. "But I have no intention of letting such a beautiful and historical structure be destroyed."

"Well," Jason cleared his throat again, and shifted his hand from his hip to the butt of his gun. "I guess that's settled then."

"It is," Suzie replied and quirked a thin brow as she tried to figure out exactly what his intentions were. In her experience as a journalist she had found she had a talent for reading people, but Jason was a very difficult read. She couldn't tell if he was angry, bored, or just emotionally repressed.

"I think you might be taking on a bigger project than you realize," he added with warning in his tone. "But like I said, anything you need, just give me a call."

"Thank you," Suzie replied as she smiled at him. "Would you like to join us for breakfast?" she offered.

"Oh I can't, I'm on duty," Jason shrugged and then smiled. "Thanks anyway." As he turned to walk away, Suzie noticed the sway in his step. She could tell that he had a very important role in the town by the way the other patrons in the diner looked up at him when he passed by them. He paused at the doorway of the diner and glanced back over his shoulder.

"Suzie, this place is a little different to the big city," he said calmly. "Remember to call me, for anything," he added as he met her eyes. Suzie was a little unsettled with the way his blue eyes seemed to bore into her own. Then he was gone, yet again without blinking an eye.

Suzie watched through the window as he started to walk across the street to his patrol car. Before he could step off the sidewalk a sleek, black sedan pulled up in front of him. He paused a moment, then the driver got out of the sedan, walked around it, and opened the rear door for

Jason. She watched him place his hand on the butt of his gun again, but just for a moment, before he slid into the back seat of the car. The driver closed the door behind him, and the sleek sedan pulled away from the sidewalk.

When Suzie returned to the table where Mary was nursing her coffee, she felt a little confused.

"Handsome cousin," Mary said with a smile and a wink as she gestured to the waitress to bring Suzie's coffee.

"Strange is more like it," Suzie said with a slow shake of her head. "I can't help but get the feeling that there is an awful lot going on in this town, just under the surface."

"Here we go," Mary said with an affectionate roll of her eyes. "Once an investigator, always an investigator."

"Oh foo," Suzie waved her hand with a laugh. "I haven't worked in a long time, Mary, you know that. The days of me hunting down the story are over."

"Sure, I can see that," Mary joked and finished the last sip of her coffee just as the waitress came to refill it.

"It seems he wants the place torn down," Suzie shrugged a little. "At first I felt badly about inheriting the property, but now I'm rather glad I did. At least we'll give it a chance to survive."

"Speaking of surviving, we better stock up on provisions before we get to work," Mary said quickly. "I spotted a grocery store in the middle of town, we should go by before we head back to the house."

"Good idea," Suzie agreed. "But first, we eat!" she said as she opened up the breakfast menu.

Suzie soon discovered that what the little town lacked in culture it more than made up for in the food it served. She hadn't had anything so tasty in a very long time. She pretended not to know that it was the ample amounts of butter and grease that made it so delicious. As she settled the bill with the waitress Suzie could feel the eyes of some of the locals on her. She smiled at the waitress.

"We'll see you again soon," she said.

"Oh, you're staying?" the waitress asked with surprise. She had curly, white hair that was poofed just enough to make her head resemble a turned dandelion. "I thought you might be just passing through."

"No, we'll be staying for a little while," Suzie said as Mary walked up beside her. "And with the delicious coffee you have I'm sure we'll be back for more."

"Okay then," the waitress smiled, her eyes gleaming with the information she'd received. "It's about time that dusty old place had some real life in it again."

"We'll do our best," Suzie laughed before she and Mary walked out the door of the diner.

***

Despite their excited chatter on the way back to the house, when Suzie took another look at the house and all of the help it needed, she felt the wind leave her sails a bit. She didn't want to invest a lot of time and money into something that couldn't be repaired. She frowned as she tested some of the wood on the porch.

"I think this will all have to be replaced," she muttered.

"Don't worry about that now," Mary reminded her. "One room at a time."

From the threadbare, dust-infested curtains to the carpet worn so thin that the bare, wooden floor could be seen beneath it, there was a lot of work to be done. Suzie and Mary were eager to get started.

"Operation sunlight!" Mary declared and began pulling down all of the old curtains. The rooms that had once been dreary and strangled by shadows were illuminated by the bright sunlight that poured in through the windows. Windows that were in dire need of some cleaning themselves.

"It seems as if my uncle just gave up," Suzie said quietly as she tugged a cover off a majestic, old piano that appeared to have been hidden in the corner for many years.

"He was just living between his bedroom and the kitchen, from what I can tell," Mary said quietly as she pressed one of the keys on the piano to see if it was in tune. The sound the piano emitted was jarring, but still seemed to fill the room with a sense of hope.

"Can you even imagine?" Suzie said as she shook her head. "My entire condo could fit in this living room. He had all of this space, and didn't use any of it."

"It must have been lonely to live here after his wife died," Mary said as she glanced around at the floor to ceiling windows and the large fireplace in the center of the living room. "Having space isn't always a luxury," she added. "I remember when my oldest left home for college, standing in the middle of his room and thinking how empty it was."

"But people leave an impression, and even when they've moved on, it still remains," Suzie said as she flipped through some of the music books hidden inside the piano bench. "The more I learn about old buildings and homes, the more I long to protect them from destruction. Once someone lives there, it's not just walls and a roof any more, is it?"

"This place certainly isn't," Mary said with a small smile of affection as she ran her fingertip along a carving in one of the walls. "You know these marks were probably to measure someone's height. It might not have even been Jason's, could have been some other little boy or girl who once lived here."

"We'll have to learn what we can about the place while we're here," Suzie suggested. "All right, let's move this furniture out of here so we can see what we can do about this carpet."

They worked together to move the furniture, most of which was rather heavy. Then Suzie crouched down and began tugging at one corner of the carpet. When she pulled on it, the carpet disintegrated in her hands.

"Hmm," she said as she glanced over at Mary. "I think we might need a little help with this."

"I think you're right," Mary laughed and laid her hand on the mantle above the fireplace. When she did she touched the glossy surface of a photograph.

"Suzie, look at this," Mary said with a smile as she picked up the photograph.

"What is it?" Suzie asked and stood up,

dusting off bits of carpet as she did.

"It's a photograph of the sunrise over the beach," Mary said with admiration as she showed it to Suzie. "It's not dusty so it was probably taken recently. If your uncle took it, he must have been a good photographer, don't you think?"

"I'd say so," Suzie replied in a murmur as she studied the image. The myriad of colors sprawled across the sky were interrupted only by a few sea birds soaring by. "It's beautiful," she admitted.

"Let's get started on this carpet," Mary coaxed her. "In no time we'll have this place looking as wonderful as it once did."

Suzie had a hard time believing that, but she was grateful for Mary's optimism. They worked together to tear up and roll back some of the carpet. Suzie was inspecting the hard wood floor, wondering if she could just polish it or if it would need to be redone, when she noticed something strange about some of the floorboards.

"Look at this," Suzie said as she traced her fingertips along the thin wood. "I don't think this is sealed," she frowned as she narrowed her eyes.

"It isn't, look here," Mary said and pulled a corner of the wood up out of the floor. It was a large square, all one piece that could be lifted out of the rest of the floorboards.

"What's underneath it?" Suzie asked with excitement creeping into her voice.

"I think it's a safe," Mary said as she looked down at the metal container with a padlock on the front.

"Wow," Suzie grinned as she reached into the hole the safe was hidden in and rocked it a little to see if it was loose. "I think I can lift it right out..." she started to say and then lifted the safe out of the hole. She set it down on the floor next to her.

"It's not too heavy," she said as she tugged at the padlock on the front. "But I don't think we're getting in here too easily."

"I think I spotted some bolt cutters in the hall closet," Mary said and hurried off to get them. When she returned with the bolt cutters Suzie hesitated.

"Do you think we should open it?" she asked with a frown.

"All of the contents belongs to you," Mary reminded her.

"I know, but it still feels strange," Suzie admitted. "I guess it wouldn't do any harm to see what's inside."

It took a few attempts but she managed to cut through the lock. When they opened the safe they found very little inside. There were a few stacks of legal papers as well as a small key.

"What do you think this belongs to?" Suzie asked as she held the key up to the sunlight drifting through the windows.

"Only key I've seen like that belonged to a safety deposit box I had," Mary said as she studied the key as well. "It looks like it might have the initials of the bank on it."

"Here, look at this," Suzie said as she pointed to one of the papers in one of the stacks. "It lists the bank and box number."

"How interesting. It seems like a lot of effort just to keep a key safe," Mary said thoughtfully. "I wonder what's inside the safety deposit box."

"Well, whatever is inside the safety deposit

box would surely belong to Jason, so I guess I should call him and let him know that we found the key," Suzie suggested with a slight shrug as she fiddled with the business card that Jason had given her.

Despite the fact they were cousins, Suzie felt a little uncomfortable around Jason. If only she could pin down his intentions, and read him as easily as she could other people, she might feel a little more secure.

"You give him a call, and I'll finish rolling up the rest of this carpet," Mary offered as she brushed some dust off the knees of her jeans.

"I don't want you doing all the work, Mary," Suzie warned as she glanced guiltily over at her friend.

"Suzie, this is the best thing for me," Mary assured her as she got back down on her knees to roll the carpet. "I've always found focusing on a task to be the best time to sort through things in my mind. It just seems easier to figure things out while my body is busy doing other things."

"Just don't overdo it," Suzie warned her as she pulled out her cell phone.

"I'm not dead yet," Mary winked at her. "In fact, for the first time in a very long time, I feel very alive."

Suzie smiled at that. It reassured her to think that something about all the work they were doing was creating some kind of healing for Mary. As Suzie dialed the number on the business card she stepped outside onto the wraparound porch to make the call. As she walked around behind the large building she found herself awestruck by the deep blue of the water against the pale blue of the sky. It seemed to grab the core of her and give it a sharp shake to see something so beautiful. It wasn't that she hadn't seen beautiful things before, but the combination of the salty air, and distant intangible memories of her youth was a powerful force.

"Hello?" Jason's voice jarred her from her thoughts. She blinked twice before she even remembered that she had called him.

"Hi, Jason it's Suzie," she paused a moment and then added. "Your cousin."

"I remember," Jason chuckled a little into

the phone. "What can I help you with?"

Suzie smiled at the question. It was endearing for someone to automatically offer to help.

"Actually, I think I have something that might help you," Suzie replied as she flipped the business card between her fingers. "Mary and I were pulling up the carpets in the living room and we came across a hidden safe. Did you know about that?"

"A hidden safe?" Jason repeated hesitantly. "I've never known my father to have a safe."

"Well, it was there," Suzie replied. "Inside were only some documents regarding the property and some old vehicles, but also a key to a safety deposit box."

"Oh?" Jason's voice had dropped in tone quite a few octaves.

"Well, your father left the contents of the house to me, but I'm sure he intended for you to have whatever was in the safe and the deposit box that this key must open," she explained. "So, would you like to come pick it up?"

"Uh, at the house?" he asked, his voice still awkward.

"If you don't mind," Suzie replied with a touch of confusion. "I'm covered in dust and carpet fibers, so I'm not exactly presentable to the public. If you'd rather I could meet you somewhere later after I've had time to clean myself up."

"No," he paused a long moment and Suzie wondered if the call might have been dropped. Right when she was about to check the connection, he spoke up. "I'll come over," he replied reluctantly as if it was the worst thing he could imagine. "Just, do me a favor and meet me outside, okay?"

"Sure, Jason," she replied with a softer voice. "Just text me when you get here."

"I will," he replied before hanging up.

Suzie stared down at the phone for a moment. She found it very odd that Jason was so opposed to stepping into the house. She had just been marvelling over the beauty that could be seen from the porch she was standing on, but Jason acted as if he'd rather be anywhere else on earth. She could understand that since his father had recently passed in the home there might be some underlying grief that caused his dislike of the place, but still, something seemed off about it. When she walked back into the living room she found that Mary had already rolled up the remainder of the carpet.

"Wow!" Suzie exclaimed with a laugh, her blue eyes dancing as they swept over the bare wooden floors. "If I had known you could do all this yourself I would have been sitting on the porch with an iced tea."

"Ha, ha," Mary panted out as she struggled to her feet. "I think I might have overestimated the youth of my back."

"Well, then it's to the porch with you, young lady," Suzie said sternly. "I'll bring you some iced tea. You will not believe the view," she sighed with pleasure at the recollection of it.

"Did you talk to Jason?" Mary asked as she dusted off her hands.

"Yes," Suzie replied and bit her lip lightly as she wondered if she should share how strange she found her cousin. "He's going to come by to pick up the key," she finally said. She didn't want to continue to question Jason's behavior. He had just lost his father after all, and had no mother to turn to either. In fact, in Suzie's estimation, she was probably Jason's closest living relative. She didn't want to alienate him just because he wasn't grieving the way she expected him to. "Go on out," Suzie encouraged Mary. "I'll meet you out there."

When Suzie stepped out onto the porch with a glass of tea in each hand, she found Mary gazing with a dreamy smile on her lips at the ocean stretched out before her.

"How could anyone give this up?" she asked quietly as she accepted the glass of tea from Suzie. "I think I could stare at the ocean forever."

Suzie rubbed her friend's back lightly and smiled sympathetically at her. "I know this is still hard for you, Mary," she said gingerly. "I can't tell you how much I appreciate your help."

"I can't tell you how much I appreciate being here," Mary replied as she took a sip of her tea. "You always seem to know exactly what to do."

"Ha," Suzie rolled her eyes at that and leaned

against the railing of the porch, with her back to the ocean. "If only that was the case," she smiled as nostalgia flooded her. There were a lot of turns in the road of her life that she would have preferred to have led down different paths. But as she glanced over her shoulder at the rolling waves and the slowly setting sun, she was certain that despite the missteps, she had landed exactly where she was meant to.

"Hello?" Jason's strong voice called from around the corner of the house. Suzie straightened up and set her glass of tea down on the flat surface of the wide railing. She walked towards the sound of Jason's voice.

"We're back here," she called out as she walked around the corner of the house to meet him. Jason stood tentatively at the edge of the porch as if he expected the wooden boards to collapse beneath him. "I thought you were going to text me?" Suzie reminded him.

"I did," he replied with a gruff edge to his voice. Suzie slid her hand into her pocket to check her phone. When she found it empty she realized that she must have left it on the kitchen counter while she was fixing the iced tea.

"Sorry, Jason," she frowned as she met his stolid blue eyes. He only looked back at her expectantly. She gritted her teeth as she realized getting the slightest hint of emotion out of him was going to be like pulling teeth. "Here," she handed him the key that she had stowed in her other pocket. "I'd be happy to give you the other paperwork that was in the safe."

Jason stared nervously at the key he was holding between his thumb and first finger. "Honestly, I don't even want this," he shrugged and started to turn away. "I'll probably just tell the bank to donate whatever is inside."

"Jason, wait," Suzie reached out and grabbed his forearm gently. He seemed a little startled by her touch, and she was just as surprised by it. Despite Jason being about the age that her own child might be if she had one, she had never felt a maternal pull before. Something about Jason made her want to understand him, and even help him if she could. Perhaps it was because they were family, or maybe it was some irrational need that she hadn't put a finger on yet.

"I just want you to know that if you need to talk," she smiled awkwardly, "I'm here. I mean, there may be some things you want out of the house. Things that belonged to your father, or to your mother," she suggested. She caught sight of a flicker of emotion cross his face when she mentioned his mother.

"There's not," he said sternly and drew his arm from her grasp. "Listen, I appreciate the gesture," he said calmly as he met her eyes. "But I have people I can talk to. Really the best thing for me would be to have all of this off my back. Okay?" he narrowed his eyes slightly as if he was willing to speak in a harsher tone if she pushed him.

"Okay," Suzie nodded slowly, though she wasn't sure if she understood. As he walked away, Suzie could tell from the tension in his shoulders that she had ruffled some feathers. She was ready to believe that Jason was one mystery she was not going to be able to figure out.

"Well, isn't he pleasant," Mary said as she walked up behind Suzie with her glass of iced tea. Suzie laughed a little as she took the glass of tea and they both watched Jason climb into his patrol car.

"Well, he is a police officer, maybe he just has to have a tough attitude," Suzie shrugged.

"Hmm, I don't think so," Mary said as she watched Jason tear out of the driveway. "I've seen that look plenty of times. He's hiding something."

"You think?" Suzie asked with surprise.

"All I'm saying is that if I ever saw that look on my son's face, I knew that we were going to need to have a long conversation," Mary laughed lightly and then arched an eyebrow. "I guess they never grow out of it."

"I guess not," Suzie replied with a slight frown. "All right, enough work for tonight I think," she grinned. "How about I start a fire and we trade in these teas for some wine?"

"Sounds like a good plan to me," Mary agreed.

***

Once the fire was crackling in the large fireplace, which was in the center of the large living room, Mary sprawled out across one of the three couches in the room. Suzie had found a box of trinkets in the master bedroom and was sorting through them in front of the fireplace.

"These must have been Beverly's," Suzie said softly as she sorted through the collection of handmade crafts. "It's sweet that he kept them for so long."

"How can Jason not want any of these things?" Mary asked with a sigh.

"I'm not going to get rid of them. I'll box them up for him, maybe one day he'll want them," Suzie said quietly. Then she paused as she pulled out an envelope from the box. "Hmm," she glanced up at Mary. "Do you think it would be wrong to read it?"

"Not at all," Mary sat up so she could listen.

When Suzie opened the envelope she expected it to be correspondence between husband and wife, but the letter she skimmed over had nothing to do with that. It was a letter from a father to a son.

"I know dear boy that we have been separated by time and hurt, and I am guilty of always believing that tomorrow would come. However, due to recent discoveries I have made, I fear my time is much shorter than I anticipated. In fact, I fear I no longer believe in tomorrow. I have felt someone watching me, and I know that I have crossed a terrible line. A funny thing happens when you are faced with the end of your life. You begin to think about all the ways you missed out on living it. When your mother died, Jason, I missed an opportunity to be the father you needed me to be. Since then I have missed that opportunity with each and every day that passed. There isn't time left to express all that I truly feel, but the most important thing that I have failed to convey for so many years, is that I love you. I ask for your forgiveness, without the expectation that it will be given. I ask for it so that you will know that I recognized the hurt that I have caused. All I ask of you is that you find a way to heal and let go of the past. Don't be an old man, in an old house, with an old mind. Live your life, Jason, with freedom and passion."

"Wow," Mary murmured as she listened intently. She smiled fondly at the familiar desire that a parent has for a child, that their lives will somehow be better than that of their parents. "What else does it say?" she asked eagerly.

"Nothing," Suzie whispered as she looked over the letter once more. "It's almost as if he planned to write more, but never had the chance to," she frowned as she tucked the paper back inside the envelope. "I'll have to make sure Jason has the chance to read this."

"I hope he will," Mary said gently and swept her gaze over the grand living room that was painted in subtle reflections of the flame in the fireplace. "I can't imagine how lonely Harry must have felt in his last days."

"But how did he know they were his last days?" Suzie asked thoughtfully. "He says that he made recent discoveries about his life coming to an end."

"Maybe a medical diagnosis?" Mary suggested with a slight shrug.

"Maybe," Suzie hesitated and then shook her head slowly. "Something just doesn't seem right about the tone of the letter. It feels as if he was afraid, not so much of a medical issue, but of a person."

"A person?" Mary scooted to the edge of the couch to look more closely at Suzie. "What makes you think that?"

"I don't know," Suzie shook her head. "Maybe I'm just reading too much into it."

"Well, no matter what inspired him to write the letter, the fact that he did is a treasure. Jason should get some relief from this, if not now, hopefully in the future," Mary murmured and then stretched her arms above her head as she yawned.

"Yes, it sounds like Beverly's death really tore Jason and his father apart. How sad to think that at a time when they needed each other the most, they were isolated from one another," she glanced over at Mary just as she was finishing her yawn. "I second that," she laughed as she stifled her own yawn. "Let's get some good rest."

They had chosen bedrooms to stay in earlier in the day. The rooms in the home had been quite neglected, but at one time it was clear that a good amount of care had been taken to select decorations and paint colors. Each room had its own theme from nautical, to whimsical, to medieval. It was only noticeable if close attention was paid to the subtle decorations and nuances of the texture of the bedding and walls. They chose two rooms close to each other, as the house was rather spooky in the dark. Suzie chose a room that had a Victorian feel to it with thick, long curtains and a four poster bed. Mary chose a room that had a more Mediterranean theme, with bright colors and simplistic furnishings. Neither of them noticed the décor in either room by the time they fell into bed, exhausted from all the hard work they had done.

Chapter Four

When Suzie's eyes fluttered open the next morning she felt as if she was floating. There was something liberating about being away from home without any set date of return. She found herself looking up at the ceiling beyond the four posts that towered above her bed. The ceiling was weathered but strong and could use a fresh coat of paint. Before she was even up for the day she was already planning what they would attack next in the refurbishing. She walked to the door of her bedroom and listened, but only heard silence. She expected that Mary was still sleeping.

As Suzie stepped into the bathroom attached to the bedroom she could feel the hard work of the day before in the muscles of her upper arms and the strain of her lower back. She was sure that a hot shower would be a good cure for that. She wrapped her hand around the bar of the old handle and turned it. The pipe offered a loud groan and spat out a few drops of water.

"Oh no," she muttered to herself. She walked

over to the sink and turned on the water at the sink. A thin stream of water dripped out. It was obvious that there was some kind of clog in the line. As she gave up on her hot shower she realized that she would need to call a plumber to resolve this problem. She tugged on a robe over her flowing silk, white nightgown and headed back out into the living room. The scent of the fireplace filled the room, still clinging to the furnishings. It was a nice smell, but it did not compare to the heavenly aroma of coffee and toast coming from the kitchen. She found that the counter had been scrubbed, a coffee maker was hooked up and brewing, and the toaster was hard at work as well.

"Mary?" she called out with confusion growing. She had been certain that Mary was still sleeping. But when she looked out of the kitchen window she saw her dear friend standing on the porch that overlooked the water. Her shoulders were rounded, her head slightly tilted down. She seemed to be savoring her time alone. Suzie decided not to interrupt her, and instead walked over to the kitchen sink to try the water.

"It doesn't work," Mary said as she stepped

into the kitchen. "I used bottled water for the coffee maker," she added.

"Thank you so much for that," Suzie said as she cast a smile in her friend's direction. "Too bad we have plumbing problems to deal with."

"Yes," Mary sighed and shook her head. "That's one thing we can't handle on our own."

"Maybe not," Suzie agreed. "But I don't have to be a plumber to see that there is something wedged in this drain. Will you check in the hall closet, I think I saw some flashlights in there yesterday," she asked as she leaned down further trying to get a good look at what was stuck in the drain.

"Sure," Mary said as she walked out of the kitchen and to the hall closet near the entrance of the house. When she stepped back into the kitchen she had more than just a flashlight, she had a camera case in her hand.

"Look what I found," she said with a smile as she handed Suzie the flashlight.

"A camera?" Suzie guessed with a slight smile.

"Not just any camera," Mary corrected her. "This is a very expensive model. Your uncle must have been a good photographer."

"From that photo on the mantle, I'd agree," Suzie murmured as she shone the flashlight down into the drain. "Hmm," she frowned.

"Can we get it out?" Mary wondered as she glanced over at Suzie.

"We're going to try," Suzie replied. Then she began searching around for something that would allow her to fish the object out. She found an old knife sharpener that seemed to be the right size. After wriggling it around for a little bit and muttering under her breath each time she thought she had it, the object slid out of her grasp once more, until she was finally able to pull it up and out of the drain. Once it was out however, it didn't solve any mysteries. It only offered more questions.

"It's a cufflink," Suzie said as she turned the circular metal object slowly between her fingers. In big, bold, black letters on the surface of the golden cufflink the initials TR stood out.

"Weird," Mary mumbled as she peered at the

cufflink. "But with the long history this place has, I'm sure that we will find many more surprises."

"Either way, we still need to get a plumber out here," Suzie said firmly. She pulled out her cell phone and slid the cufflink into her pocket. She would take a closer look at it later just out of curiosity. Once she set up a time for the plumber to come out, she began thinking about the letter she had found the day before. She was wondering if she should call Jason and give it to him when her cell phone began to ring. She saw that it was Jason calling in.

"Hi Jason, I was just thinking about calling you," Suzie said quickly.

"Can you meet me at the bank?" Jason rushed forward in a quiet tone.

Suzie was surprised by the sudden change in the tone of his voice. All of the certainty and logic that had coursed through his words before seemed to have vanished.

"Of course, I'll be there in a few minutes," Suzie replied. "Is everything okay?"

"Everything is fine," he assured her. "Just meet me as soon as you can."

"Okay," Suzie agreed and hung up the phone. "Mary, do you think you could handle the plumber while I meet Jason in town?"

"Sure, no problem," Mary nodded as she continued to shine the flashlight down the sink. "Just wondering if the other one is down there, too," she laughed.

***

When Suzie arrived at the bank, Jason was standing outside. It was the first time Suzie had seen him without his uniform, and in jeans and a t-shirt he looked much younger than she had first assumed.

"Hi there," she smiled as she walked up to him. Jason didn't smile back, he glanced up at her nervously instead.

"I couldn't open the box," he said quietly and lowered his eyes.

"Oh Jason, I'm sorry, was it too difficult for you?" she asked with a frown.

"No," he replied darkly. "My father left a

specific note with the manager of the bank, that I should not open the box. He named you as the only person who could open the box."

"Me?" Suzie asked with a shake of her head. "This is getting a little ridiculous."

"Not to me it isn't," Jason said and narrowed his eyes. "This is how he always was. He kept things inside. When my mother died I was away on vacation and he waited almost two days to tell me. Two days of me living my life and enjoying myself, having no idea that..." his voice broke slightly and he shook his head. "Obviously he didn't trust me with whatever is in that box, so here," he handed her the key. Suzie took it and then studied him intently.

"Do you want to come inside with me?" she offered awkwardly. She had no idea how to react to her uncle's dismissal of his son. She wished she could give the letter she had found to Jason, but she didn't feel as if that moment was the right time. The last thing she wanted was for Jason to throw the letter into the trash without reading it.

"No," he sighed and then rocked back on his

heels. "I'm going to go to the diner and have a nice early lunch, and forget about all of this. Good luck," he added and turned to walk down the sidewalk.

Suzie stepped into the bank. She hated to think of Jason feeling so hurt, but she was very curious about what might be in the safety deposit box.

When she walked into the bank, the woman behind the counter was smiling in the direction of the door, as if she was waiting for Suzie to enter. Suzie returned the smile, though she was still a little troubled. As she walked up to the curved front counter the woman laid a clipboard with some forms clipped to it in front of Suzie.

"You must be Suzie Allen," she said swiftly. "I just need you to fill out these forms, and I'll need to see some identification."

Suzie nodded and began filling in her information on the form. When she finished she handed the woman her ID and then glanced around the bank. It was a quiet place with thick carpets and floor to ceiling double paned glass windows. It had a sterile feel to it, but the atmosphere was courteous.

"All set, Ms. Allen," the woman said as she returned to the counter. "If you'll follow me," she opened a small gate in the counter so that Suzie could step through. They walked down a long, narrow hallway to a secure room where the safety deposit boxes were stored. The teller walked over to the wall of safety deposit boxes, found the number that belonged to Harry's, and pointed it out to Suzie.

"I'll leave you to look through the contents, please let me know if there's anything you need," she said as she walked back out of the door.

Suzie stared at the box, then unlocked it with the key. She slid the metal container out from inside the small space, and carried it to the large wooden table in the center of the room. As she opened the lock on the box, she wondered what would be inside. What she found left her very surprised. Though the box was fairly large and could have contained several different things there was only a single envelope in the bottom of it. It was a thick envelope and felt heavy when Suzie picked it up. She opened the envelope to discover a pile of photographs inside and a USB flash drive.

Suzie lifted the photographs out of the envelope. She laid them in a pile on the table beside the box. When she looked inside she discovered that the photographs and the drive were the only things that the envelope had contained. Puzzled, she looked back at the photographs. She expected to see a young Jason playing with his mother, or even some boudoir photographs of Beverly, something that someone would treasure enough to pay for a safety deposit box to keep them safe.

Suzie picked up the first photograph and stared down at it closely. What she saw were two strangers standing on the beach at night. The man held a bottle of wine in one hand, and was dressed in a nice suit. Beside him the woman was dressed in a butter yellow, flowing dress. She was bare foot, with her white sandals clutched in one hand. She was looking up at him, smiling. It felt like a special night between lovers. The man looked to be in his late forties or fifties, and the woman seemed a bit younger.

In the next photo they were strolling along the beach, their arms entangled with one another. In the next photo they were standing about a foot from one another. The man's expression was grim, filled with arrogance and power. The woman appeared to be frightened with widened eyes. Suzie noticed she had dropped her sandals on the sand by her bare feet.

In the final photograph in the collection the woman had turned away from the man. She appeared to be in mid-motion when the photograph was snapped, as if she was trying to run from the man. He had his right hand on her right shoulder in an attempt to stop her, and still gripped the wine bottle tightly in his left. Suzie felt extremely uncomfortable.

The photographs were professional enough to have been used for some kind of advertising campaign. Perhaps there was a reason behind what seemed to be a romantic evening that turned sour. But the fear in the woman's eyes as she looked at the man towering over her left Suzie feeling sick to her stomach with dread. She gathered the photographs together and tucked them along with the flash drive back into the envelope, which she then stowed in her purse. She put the box back into its slot and then pressed the buzzer for the woman who promptly came and let her out of the room. She walked out of the bank and thought of calling Jason to tell him about what she had found, but she wondered what the point would be. Harry had been adamant about Jason not having them, perhaps because of their disturbing nature.

Suzie couldn't imagine what would possess her uncle to keep the photographs. Had he been the one to take them? She recalled the artistic photograph they had found in the living room, and the expensive camera they had found in the hall closet. It made sense that he would have been the one to take them, as the stretch of beach did seem to be similar to the beach that Dune House overlooked. However, what was the point of the photos? To record a marital spat? Surely that was all it was. The man seemed overbearing and aggressive, and the woman genuinely frightened, but that didn't mean that one moment captured on film had led to anything dire.

Chapter Five

When Suzie returned to Dune House and found Mary and the plumber talking on the porch she briefly forgot about the photographs.

"What do you think?" she asked the plumber, who had the name Lester stitched on his gray shirt. She didn't know if that was his first name or last name, and hoped she wouldn't have to use him frequently enough to find out.

"Nothing to worry about," he said with a shrug. "Just a bit of a clog, I snaked it out. If it happens again though we'll have to take a closer look at the pipes."

"Thank you for coming out at such short notice," Suzie said politely as she pulled out her check book and scribbled out a check for the amount Mary pointed out on the bill of service.

"No trouble," he shrugged again. "Anything for this old place," he added as he looked over his shoulder affectionately at the large structure. "It's good to see someone finally trying to work to improve it," he added with a smile.

Suzie smiled in return as she handed him the check. It was nice to know that Dune House was still valued by some residents in the town. After Lester left, Suzie recalled the photographs in her purse.

"Boy do I have a strange story to tell you," she said as she followed Mary into the house.

"What happened at the bank?" Mary asked eagerly.

"You wouldn't believe it but Jason could not access the box. Uncle Harry left strict instructions that I was the only one allowed to open it," Suzie explained.

"Wow," Mary gasped. "What was in it?"

"The only things in the box were these photographs," Suzie replied as she set the stack of photographs down on the large dining room table that they had yet to polish, "and this flash drive." She took the flash drive out of the envelope and showed it to Mary and then put it in her pocket. They didn't have a computer set up yet so they would have to wait until they could look at it.

"Photographs?" Mary asked with surprise

and began to sort through them. "How strange," she murmured as she watched the scene play out in each photograph. "Why would your uncle want to keep these safe?"

"I don't know," Suzie shook her head. "I was thinking I should show them to Jason and see if he knows the people in the photographs."

"Suzie," Mary said softly as she studied the photo of the man grabbing onto the woman's shoulder. "Look at his cufflink," she said as she pointed to it.

Suzie leaned closer to take a look. "It does look similar to the one we found," Suzie said quietly as she studied the photograph.

"I found some knick-knacks in one of the kitchen drawers," Mary said as she walked into the kitchen. She opened one of the drawers and pulled out a magnifying glass. "Do you still have the cufflink?" Mary asked as she handed Suzie the magnifying glass.

"Yes, I do," Suzie replied and fished it out of her pocket. She laid it on the table so they could both take a closer look at it. Then Suzie leaned over the photo with the magnifying glass. As she held the magnifying glass over the photograph she could swear that she saw initials on the man's cufflink, but she couldn't quite make out the letters. She frowned as she glanced up at Mary.

"I think there is a lot more to my uncle's death than we are seeing," she shook her head slowly. "At first I thought it was just my suspicious nature getting the better of me, but now I'm certain. Something happened to my uncle, and I don't think it was a death of natural causes."

"What do you see in the photograph?" Mary asked curiously.

"I can't quite see it," Suzie admitted. "But I think the man in this photo is wearing the same cufflinks."

"If only there was a way that we could see the cufflinks up close," Mary frowned as she scrutinized the photograph through the magnifying glass as well. When she brushed her hand across the cherry wood table, she came back with a palm full of dust.

"I think we had better get to work on some of

this cleaning," Suzie suggested as she tucked the photographs back into the envelope. "It'll give me some time to sort things out."

"Good idea," Mary agreed. "I'll start with the windows so we can get some more light in here."

"I'm going to work on the furniture," Suzie nodded. As the two women set to work, Suzie's mind sorted through all that she had discovered over the past few days. One question bothered her, why was it that her uncle didn't leave these clues to his own son, who was a police officer after all. If he had stumbled across something potentially criminal or dangerous, why hadn't he turned to Jason?

"This is odd, Suzie," Mary called out as she stood in the window that overlooked the beach below.

"What?" Suzie asked and walked over to her.

"See how filthy the windows are?" Mary pointed out. "All but this one patch here," she pointed to a perfectly clean, smudge-free section of the glass.

"Huh," Suzie said thoughtfully. Suddenly she thought of something and hurried back to the envelope to grab the photographs. She held one of the photographs up to the clean patch on the window.

"Looks like it could be the same angle," Mary said thoughtfully.

"So, it was Harry who took these photos," Suzie said with a shake of her head. "He must have taken them from here. What was he seeing that was so important to him?"

"Maybe it was just the emotions they were displaying," Mary suggested. "Perhaps he thought of it as an interesting photographic opportunity."

"Yes," Suzie nodded a little. "That's possible. I can see that the first photo would capture an artist's interest. I'm not sure what to think about the rest."

"Well, I can tell you this much, the cleaner I have on hand is not going to get these windows clean. I think we need to go into town for some more heavy duty supplies," she frowned.

"All right, we could use a break anyway," Suzie shrugged. "Maybe we can get some coffee at the diner."

"Anything to get my mind off Kent's phone calls," Mary sighed as she followed her friend out the door.

"Has he been calling you again?" Suzie asked with surprise. It was the first her friend had mentioned it.

"Yes, he's insisting on knowing where I am, and what I'm doing, and when I'll be back. I just sent him a text to inform him that he no longer needed to know those things once he filed for divorce," she rolled her eyes and shook her head. "Never again, Suzie. I know you tried to tell me the first time, but please, if you see me falling head over heels for someone just smack me."

"I promise," Suzie laughed as they drove towards the center of town. A part of Suzie felt a little saddened, however. Despite having many boyfriends over the years Suzie had never met a man who she was interested in spending more than a few weeks with. She couldn't comprehend the idea of inviting someone into her life on a permanent basis. She chalked it up to her being a private person, but sometimes she wondered if she was missing out on something. After seeing what Kent had put Mary through, it was hard for her to believe that any relationship was worth that kind of pain.

When they reached the hardware store to pick up some cleaning items and other supplies, Suzie did her best to put those thoughts out of her mind, and cheer her friend up instead.

"Look, Mary, a new hairstyle?" she suggested as she plopped a bright blue mop on the top of her head.

"Hmm, I like the color, the texture not so much," Mary laughed out loud. The owner of the hardware store eyed them warily from the counter.

"Watch out now," Suzie called out before firing a few sponges in Mary's direction.

"Suzie!" Mary huffed as she picked up the sponges. Instead of setting them back on the shelf however, she threw them right back. Soon the two were giggling and avoiding the disapproving glare of the store owner. It felt like they were kids again, finding any way possible to have fun. Suzie noticed that it chased away some of the sorrow from Mary's warm brown eyes. By the time they had all the supplies they needed the store owner was more than happy to see them go.

Mary and Suzie were still giggling to each other when they stepped out of the hardware store. Suzie was startled when she saw the same black sedan she had seen at the diner before, parked right behind her own car. A man was standing beside the car, dressed in a very nice suit, his wavy, gray hair swept back neatly. Jason, in full uniform, was standing in front of him on the sidewalk and they seemed to be talking very heatedly about something.

"Jason?" Suzie called out as she walked towards him. Mary took the bags that Suzie was carrying from her so that her hands would be free.

"Not now," Jason said darkly as he glanced over at her and then back at the man before him.

"Jason," the man said in a disapproving paternal tone. "Don't be rude."

Jason narrowed his eyes and glanced down at the sidewalk as if he wasn't sure what to do. Suzie didn't like the way the man was looking at her younger cousin, as if Jason had to answer to him.

"Hello, I'm Suzie, Jason's cousin," Suzie explained quickly as she held out her hand to the man. She noticed a flicker of heat in his eyes before he extended his own hand and accepted hers with a polite handshake.

"Pleasure to meet you, Suzie," he said quietly. "Sorry to keep Jason from you, but a mayor's job never ends," he chuckled and released her hand. Suzie glanced over at Jason who was standing uncomfortably beside them both.

"Mayor?" she asked with surprise when she looked back at the man before her.

"I'm sorry, it was rude of me not to introduce myself," he shook his head and smiled. "I'm Thomas Ralley, mayor of this fine town," he added and winked at Suzie. Suzie smiled in response to his wink, but her eyes naturally narrowed with suspicion.

"I've been looking for an opportunity to introduce myself," he added with a shy grin. "I just didn't know when would be the right time. You two ladies have been quite busy, I've heard," he added as he looked over Suzie's shoulder at Mary who still had her arms full of the cleaning supplies they had just purchased.

"Quite," Suzie agreed and felt her smile fade slightly. "I'm glad to have met you, Mr. Ralley," she added.

"Oh please, call me Tom, everyone does," he chuckled and glanced over at Jason. "Must be nice having family in town, Jason," he said in a mild tone.

"Very," Jason spoke shortly and then cleared his throat. "I've tried to convince her that the house is a total loss, but she's determined," he raised an eyebrow as he looked directly at Suzie. Suzie felt the tension rise in the middle of the conversation though she could not place why it was there. Something about Thomas made her very uncomfortable, as if she'd met him before and had a reason not to like him.

"Well, we can't give up so easily on things just because they're a little aged," she chuckled a little. "I suppose it's hard for someone as young as you to understand that Jason."

Jason pursed his lips and glanced away

dismissively.

"Jason is one of our finest officers," Thomas offered to smooth out the feathers that seemed to have been ruffled. "Without him our police force would never run as well. He's pretty good at not giving up," he added and then lowered his voice with a playful tone. "I like to think he gets that from me."

"Oh?" Suzie asked with surprise as she looked between Jason and Thomas. "Do you know each other well?"

"He's a family friend," Jason said quickly and then laid a hand lightly on Mary's shoulder. "Let me help you with those," he offered as he took some bags from her.

"I would love to have dinner," Thomas suggested as Jason was steering Mary in the direction of the car. He paused and tossed a glance in the direction of the mayor.

"I'm sure they'll be tired..." Jason began to say, but Suzie interrupted him.

"I'd really enjoy that," Suzie said with a shrug, she wanted to know just how much influence this man had on her cousin. "Do you have a place in mind?"

"Cheney's has the best pasta in town," Thomas smiled as he glanced from Suzie to Mary who was getting into the car. Jason was still staring hard at Thomas. "Say about seven?" he suggested. "Jason, you should join us," he said, his voice gaining a sterner tone.

"Well, I..."

"Oh, that would be lovely," Suzie said with a broad smile. "We could use the break, and I feel like I haven't had the chance to learn anything about the town, or my cousin," she added as she looked over at Jason. Jason lowered his eyes and nodded reluctantly.

"See you then," Thomas smiled and turned to walk away from the car.

"Are you okay, Jason?" Suzie asked as she walked towards the driver's side door of the car.

"I'd be better if you had just taken my advice," he said rather shortly as he met her eyes across the top of the car.

"Is there something you want to tell me, Jason?" Suzie asked calmly. He held her gaze for a long moment as if he was considering it, but finally he looked away and closed the passenger side door he had been holding open for Mary.

"See you at seven," he sighed and strolled off down the sidewalk. Suzie watched him for a moment before sliding into the driver's seat. She looked over at Mary piled to her chin with bags and couldn't help but laugh.

"There is a trunk you know," she grinned as she pulled the bags off her friend and tossed them onto the back seat.

"With that conversation, I wasn't going to say a word," Mary said with a slow shake of her head. "You know, Suzie, when you first brought it up I thought you were being a little paranoid, but now that I've seen it with my own eyes, I think I agree with you."

"Agree with me about what?" Suzie asked as she started the car.

"Something isn't right with Jason, and I'm certain it has something to do with that mayor," she added through gritted teeth.

"I didn't get a good feeling about dear old Thomas either," Suzie admitted and drove back towards the house.

"Well, obviously you would be suspicious of him," Mary said with a shrug.

"What do you mean?" Suzie asked curiously.

"I mean the photograph," Mary reminded her as she looked over at Suzie. "Didn't you recognize him?"

All of a sudden Suzie's eyes widened and she drew a sharp breath. The truth was she hadn't recognized him. But the moment that Mary mentioned the photograph, she knew exactly who her friend was talking about. There was no question in her mind that the man she had just met was the very same man in the photograph they had found in the safety deposit box.

"Oh my," she whispered as they pulled into the long drive of the house. "I'm starting to think that my uncle really did get into the middle of something he shouldn't have."

Once inside the house Suzie immediately pulled out the photographs again. Sure enough the man in the photo was identical to the mayor they had just met.

"If what Jason said was true and Thomas was an old family friend, then he and Harry must have known each other," she tapped her chin slightly and shook her head. "None of this makes any sense at all to me."

"It's a little confusing," Mary agreed and pointed to the expression on the frightened woman's face. "I think it's time we found out who this person is. Was she his lover? Perhaps he was having an affair and these photos were going to prove it?"

"Do you really think my uncle would be killed over a simple affair?" Suzie asked as she picked up the photo of the woman with a clear image of her face.

"We don't know that he was killed," Mary reminded her. "Maybe he was so stressed over discovering that his friend was cheating on his wife, that he really did have a sudden heart attack."

"Maybe," Suzie said softly as she recalled the firm grip of the mayor's handshake. "Thomas Ralley, TR," she shook her head and frowned. "I bet that cufflink really does belong to him."

"We have some time before dinner, maybe we should head into town and see if we can find out about the woman in the photograph?" Mary suggested as she glanced over the still messy living room. "It beats cleaning!"

"I guess you're right," Suzie nodded and then looked up at Mary. "But we should be careful who we talk to. If the mayor is as dangerous as I suspect he might be, then we don't want to make ourselves targets."

"He is dangerous," Jason said from the doorway of the house. It still startled Suzie to see him in his uniform considering her history with the police.

"Jason," she smiled at him as he stepped further inside. "We are looking forward to dinner tonight."

"Look, I don't know what the two of you think you're doing," Jason said in a cool tone that did not even pretend to be polite. "But if it involves the mayor, you need to stop. He wants this property, and if I had inherited it, I would have handed it right over to him. He is only taking you to dinner to convince you to sell the property to him," he paused a moment and looked directly into Suzie's eyes. "He is used to getting what he wants."

"Jason, did your father know Thomas well?" Suzie asked, ignoring his warning.

"Actually my mother, Beverly, knew his wife, Samantha, well," Jason reluctantly admitted. "My father and Thomas never really got along. My father was always busy," he added and narrowed his eyes. "Too busy to be there for my mother, or me. Thomas is the one that taught me to play ball, to ride a bike," he frowned and rubbed the back of his neck. "He's not the easiest man, but at least he cares."

Suzie had to bite her lip to keep from revealing the letter she had found. "Was your father always interested in photography?" she asked as she picked up the photo of the sunrise to show him. Jason barely looked at it.

"After my mother died he started taking photographs," Jason shrugged. "It was like he needed something to distract him from the truth."

"That she was gone?" Suzie coaxed him,

trying to salvage a little more information from him.

"That he wasn't there when she needed him," Jason corrected sternly. "Before she died he was obsessed with this house. He wanted it to be perfect, wanted to restore it to its historical state. Of course Thomas wanted the town to move on, to get more progressive so he and my father were always arguing over it," he glanced at his watch briefly. "I should go, I am covering someone's shift for the afternoon."

"Jason wait, stay for a little longer," Suzie suggested.

"How about a beer?" Mary offered. "There's still some in the fridge that your father must have left."

"Beer?" he raised an eyebrow. "My father didn't drink," he said firmly. "If he did, it wasn't beer."

"Oh, well I guess someone else must have left it," Mary said with a frown.

"I need to get back to work," Jason said firmly. "I only came here, because I thought it best to warn you. Thomas has influence all over this town, so if you try to restore this place you're going to be in for a real battle. I wasn't going to say anything about it, but I just didn't think it was fair to let the two of you work so hard, when he'll likely find a legal loophole to sweep it out from under you."

"Thank you for the warning, Jason," Suzie said in a warmer tone. She didn't want to alienate him, but she could tell that he was troubled by going against what Thomas wanted. She could also see a little bit of fear in his expression when he spoke of Thomas. She wondered if he had some kind of influence over Jason as a police officer, as well.

"So, I should cancel dinner?" Jason asked hopefully.

"Oh no, we'll be there," Suzie smiled sweetly. "Wouldn't miss it."

Jason rolled his eyes as his shoulders drooped. He opened his mouth as if he might have something more to say, then he just shook his head and walked back out of the house.

"He's awfully grumpy," Mary muttered as she watched the door slam behind him.

"I think it's time we unravelled just what kind of power Thomas has over Jason," Suzie said as she placed her hands on her hips. "Enough is enough, it's time to put all of this to rest. Let's head to the library, we're going to find out who that woman is in the photograph, and why the photographs are important, oh and," she snatched up the cufflink from the table, "this is coming to dinner with us tonight."

Chapter Six

Once they got to town again it was late afternoon and many of the small shops and businesses in the town were already preparing to close. Luckily, the library was still open. When they stepped in they noticed a man with stark white hair standing behind the reception desk. He wore a pair of glasses with thick lenses and was leafing through a large reference book.

"Excuse me, sir," Suzie said as she walked up to the desk.

"Yes," he asked as he peered at her over the rim of his glasses.

"I was wondering if you could help me with something," she said as she laid the photo of the woman on the desk in front of him. "I'm visiting from out of town, and I found this photo."

"Oh, I know all about you," he smiled, and when he did the stodgy demeanor that he first gave off faded into something much more mischievous. "Suzie Allen, niece of Harry and Beverly Allen, cousin to our beloved Jason

Allen," he smiled a little as he glanced over at Mary who was standing a few steps behind her. "And Mary Brent, you, I don't know as much about, my darling, but I am glad to meet you," he offered her a charming smile and a wink.

Mary managed a smile and a nod, but Suzie noticed the warmth of her expression did not warm her eyes. When she looked back at the man before her he was still smiling.

"I'm Louis," he explained as he closed the book he had been reading. "Don't worry, I'm not a stalker, I just make it my business to know everything I can about this town, and that includes long lost relatives."

"Well, then I think I am talking to the right person," Suzie smiled and pushed the photo closer to him. He glanced down at the photo, then looked back up at her with an arched eyebrow.

"You must be from out of town," he said, his voice lowering. "Put that photograph away before you get me fired."

"What? Why?" Suzie asked and glanced over at Mary who seemed just as confused. She tucked the photo back into her purse.

"Why? Because that's a photograph of Samantha, the Mayor Ralley's wife," he lowered his voice even further so that Suzie had to lean in closer to hear what he was saying. "She ran off about three weeks ago. No one knows why. The rumor is that she was upset with his less than legal behaviors, and she demanded a divorce."

"Oh," Suzie said as her heart fluttered in her chest. "And no one knows where she is?"

"No one has heard from her. She's got a sister two towns over, hasn't heard a word. She tried to get the police to look into it, but since Mayor Ralley is, well you know, mayor, they dismissed it as a marital dispute and decided not to look into it," he frowned as he glanced around the library to make sure no one else was listening in. "Last person I know for sure who saw her was Jason. He came in here upset after talking to her, asked me if I knew about some of the different members of the police force taking bribes from Ralley. I told him no of course, because Jason, as good of a kid as he's always been, has no clue what kind of man Ralley is, and I didn't trust that Jason wouldn't turn around and tell Ralley what

I said."

"And you're not worried about us doing the same?" Mary asked as she rested one elbow on the desk.

"No," he replied with a chuckle and shook his head. "No one would believe it coming from outsiders, but if Jason said it, well Jason is known to be one of the most honest people left in this town. He's a good man, a good police officer, just a little clueless when it comes to Ralley. Can't really blame him though, Ralley's been trying to take that boy's father's place ever since he found out Samantha couldn't have kids."

"Wow, you really do know about everything in this town," Suzie replied with amazement. "Is there anything you don't know?" she asked.

"I don't know how a man as healthy as Harry drops dead of a heart attack," Louis replied with a darkened gaze. Suzie was a little startled by his words. "Now, if you don't mind, I need to close up."

"Sure, thank you for your help," Suzie said quickly as she could tell that he was worried he had said more than he should have. She wanted to use one of the library computers to see what was on the flash drive but she didn't want to delay him.

"Just don't mention it, I mean that," he said sternly and waved them towards the door.

As soon as they were outside on the sidewalk Mary turned and grabbed Suzie by the elbow.

"You do know what this means?" she asked as she locked eyes with Suzie.

"Tell me what you think," Suzie encouraged her.

"If Samantha saw Jason before she disappeared and she told Jason her suspicions about Mayor Ralley maybe she also told him she was planning to leave her husband. If that's the case, then Jason probably felt terribly guilty about being with her shortly before she disappeared," she pointed out with a frown. "I bet that's why he's being very loyal to Ralley. If he's as manipulative as everyone says, he's probably got Jason completely on his side."

"Maybe," Suzie nodded as she gazed down the sidewalk at the people who were heading home for the day. "But I think Jason suspects something. I'm sure he doesn't suspect that his father might not have died of natural causes, however," she tightened her jaw.

"Do you really think that Mayor Ralley killed him?" Mary asked as she studied Suzie's expression.

"I think it's time we find out if my uncle's death was as natural as everyone seems to think," she said with determination.

"How are we going to do that?" Mary asked.

Suzie glanced at her watch. "We still have two hours before we're supposed to meet with Jason and Mayor Ralley for dinner. That should be enough time to get some information from the coroner."

"Oh Suzie, are you sure?" Mary asked as she touched her arm gently. "It won't upset you too much."

"The only way it will upset me is if I never look into it," Suzie replied with certainty. She glanced up at the fading light in the afternoon sky. "Uncle Harry trusted me with this mystery, I don't know why. Maybe he kept track of me. Maybe he knew that I had a career as an investigative journalist and he hoped that I would look deeper into things. Maybe he just wanted to protect Jason from discovering the truth. Whatever the real reason, he left this responsibility in my hands, and I intend to get to the bottom of this."

"Let's get over there then," Mary said with her shoulders squared. "Mayor or not, Ralley has no idea what he's up against when the two of us are working together."

When they reached the police station, Mary's cell phone began to ring. She glanced down at it and frowned. She sent the call to voicemail. Then the phone began to ring again.

"Ugh, I guess I better take this," Mary huffed, knowing that it was her soon to be ex-husband, Kent.

"It's fine, you wait here, that way if they cuff me you can make bail," Suzie chuckled and put the car in park. Mary was arguing on the phone with Kent when Suzie closed the door behind her. She couldn't wait for her friend to truly be free of him, but she knew that Mary had to handle it in her own way.

When she walked into the police station, Suzie felt a surge of anxiety. It had been so many years, and yet the presence of so many uniformed officers and the subtle clang of metal doors reminded her of just how it felt to have her freedom taken from her, even if for only one night. It had been hard to believe that she would ever walk out of that cell, and that had driven the point home well enough for her to avoid investigating anything so serious again. However, here she was again, about to lie through her teeth to the man at the front desk.

"Hello," Suzie smiled at him as she walked up to him.

"Hello," he replied and swept his gaze over her with curiosity. He was nearly bald with a short, stubby beard that spread awkwardly along his full drooping cheeks and rounded chin. "How can I help you?" he asked.

"My cousin, Jason Allen, is an officer here," she explained. "My uncle, Harry Allen recently passed, and I was hoping to speak to the coroner."

"Why would you need to speak to the

coroner?" he asked as his pale green eyes settled on her.

"Honestly, I just have a few personal health issues and I'd like to know if he had any of these issues at the time of his passing," she explained. "It would only take a few minutes."

"I'll see if she's free," he agreed and picked up the phone on the desk. Suzie smiled with relief. She had expected to have to lie more than that, but apparently Jason's reputation was as stellar as Louis at the library had described it.

"Sure, uh huh," the desk sergeant muttered into the phone. "All right then I'll send her down," he said, then hung up the phone. When he looked back up at Suzie his expression hadn't changed. "Just take that elevator there," he pointed to the elevator at the end of the lobby. "Hit B for Basement," he explained. "Then go down the hall and it's the third door on the right," he lowered his voice as he added. "Make sure you go right, the doors on the left, you don't want to see what's in there," he assured her.

Suzie cringed a little at the idea of what the doors on the left might be hiding. She assumed they might contain bodies. She didn't think a small town like Garber had too many murders to be concerned about, but then she wouldn't have anticipated a crooked mayor either. As she rode down on the elevator she felt her anxiety rising. She wondered if she would be able to convince the coroner to tell her the truth about her uncle's death. Was it possible that she had been bought and paid for by Mayor Ralley as well?

When she stepped off the elevator she found a dimly lit and completely empty hallway. The doors weren't even marked. There was nothing in the hallway to indicate where she should go and where she shouldn't. She counted the doors and made sure that she went to the right. When she opened the door she was greeted by a stark, medicinal scent that made her stomach churn slightly. A woman was standing over a microscope, her dark blonde hair swept up into a half-bun at the back of her head, the rest flowing down over her shoulders to reach her mid-back. When she turned to see who had stepped inside, Suzie was surprised to see how young she looked. Maybe even younger than Jason. She had soft features, and soothing hazel eyes that seemed to set Suzie at ease.

"Hello, I'm Suzie Allen," she said as she stepped further into the room.

"Ah yes, Ms. Allen, sorry," she pulled the gloves she was wearing off her hands and disposed of them in the bio-hazard container that was closest to her. "I'm Dr. Rose, I'm actually really glad to have the chance to speak with you."

"Really?" Suzie asked. "Why is that?"

"Well, we get a lot of heart attacks around here," she explained and then hesitated. "I hope that I didn't offend you."

"Not at all," Suzie said gently. "I didn't know my uncle very well."

"Well, like I've said I've seen quite a few heart attacks. This particular heart attack is a very rare one. I've never seen one myself before. The heart itself was in perfect condition prior to the attack."

"That's strange," Suzie said as she narrowed her eyes.

"Very strange," Dr. Rose agreed with a nod.

101

"Especially since these types of heart attacks are only seen in two types of people. Extreme athletes, and drug users."

"Oh," Suzie cringed as she shook her head. "I don't think my uncle was a drug user."

"I don't think so either," Dr. Rose admitted. "His liver was in good health, habitual drug use or drinking would have caused damage to his liver. I believe he might have taken a very high dose of something, however I couldn't find anything in his blood."

"Is that why you ruled his death to be of natural causes?" Suzie pried carefully.

"Yes, unfortunately, I can't prove otherwise," she paused a moment and looked into Suzie's eyes. "I can't prove it, but I do suspect otherwise. That's why I was glad to see you. I've tried to get information from Jason about his family's health history but getting two words out of that man is exhausting."

"I know what you mean," Suzie chuckled. "Well, my father did die when I was young, but it was from cancer, not a heart attack."

"Hmm, and you?" Dr. Rose asked as she

pulled out a folder with what Suzie could only assume was her uncle's medical information in it. "Have you had any problems with your heart?"

"No," Suzie shook her head slowly. "I've always been in good health, actually."

Dr. Rose made a few notes on the paperwork. In the silence, Suzie found herself wondering how someone could cause a heart attack in someone else.

"Is it possible that someone poisoned him, Dr. Rose?" she asked.

"It's possible," Dr. Rose replied hesitantly. "Like I said, I didn't find anything unusual in his system, but since it had been three days by the time we found him," her voice trailed off.

"Oh my, I didn't know about that," Suzie said with a deep frown. It was unsettling to think of her uncle being alone in that house for so long. But it made sense to her considering how reclusive her uncle had become. Jason had to feel terrible that he hadn't realized that his father was gone. He had the same experience after his mother passed.

"Yes," Dr. Rose said sadly. "Unfortunately, some of the things I could test for might have degraded in his system so much by the time that he was found, that they might not be detected."

"So, you're saying there's no way to medically prove if he was killed deliberately," Suzie said with surprise in her voice. "But everyone around town seems to think that he died of natural causes."

"Well," Dr. Rose closed the file and set it down on the desk beside the microscope she had been looking through. "You'll find in Garber that things work a little differently, Ms. Allen," she said with a hint of bitterness in her voice. "I've had to be careful not to express my opinions too loudly. But like I said, there is no proof, and so I could technically only rule his death as due to natural causes."

"Well, I appreciate your time and your candor," Suzie said as her heart skipped a beat. She knew now that she was not the only one who suspected her uncle's death had not been due to natural causes. "If you find anything, can you let me know?" she asked.

"Absolutely," Dr. Rose agreed. Then she smiled a little. "It's good to know that Jason still has family."

Suzie smiled in return. "It's been a pleasure to get to know him."

As she rode the elevator back up to the lobby of the police station, she just hoped that Jason wasn't going to end up despising her for digging so deeply into something that was a mystery to her, and a tragedy to him.

When she stepped out onto the sidewalk she found Mary waiting for her.

"I'm so sorry about that, Suzie. Kent was upset about some paper that didn't get signed," she shrugged and rolled her eyes. "There wasn't much I could do about it from here."

"It's okay," Suzie replied, still a little dazed from what Dr. Rose had revealed. "It looks like uncle Harry might have been poisoned," she said quietly.

"Poisoned?" Mary gasped.

"Shh!" Suzie grabbed her arm and steered her towards the car. "We can't let word get around that we suspect anything. At least not until I have a chance to get to know Mayor Ralley over dinner," she smirked a little before sliding into the driver's seat.

Chapter Seven

When Suzie and Mary arrived at the restaurant it was fairly busy. It appeared that most of the dinner crowd were at the tail end of their meal.

"We're waiting for two more," Suzie said as the hostess offered to seat them.

"Oh, they're already here," the young woman said quickly. "The mayor reserved his table for you," she added with a dreamy smile. Suzie and Mary exchanged glances before they were led through the restaurant. It was certainly not a five star restaurant, but you wouldn't know it from the people who were dining there. Everyone was dressed in their finest, including Jason and the mayor, both of whom stood up when the two women approached.

"Welcome," Thomas said and pulled out Suzie's chair for her. Jason did not miss a beat to do the same for Mary. Suzie tried not to be impressed by their manners, but it was hard not to be. When she sat down across from the two men, she found herself entertaining a terrible thought. If everyone was in Thomas' pocket as so many had said, then was Jason in his pocket, too? Was it possible that her cousin had something to do with his father's passing?

"What would you like to have to drink, ladies?" Thomas asked as he handed them each a menu. "Jason and I have already ordered ours," he added.

"I think I'll have a glass of wine," Mary said with a smile as the waitress approached.

"They have a delicious chardonnay here," Thomas suggested with a flash of his impossibly white teeth.

"Let's make it two," Suzie suggested and sat back as the waitress placed drinks on the table for Thomas and Jason.

Suzie had to bite into her bottom lip to keep from gasping when she saw the label on the beer that was placed down in front of Thomas.

"Your favorite, Mr. Mayor," the waitress smiled.

"Thank you so much, I have been looking forward to one of these all day," he sighed as he turned the dark, glass bottle between his palms. "Nothing like a reward after some hard work. I guess you both know all about that," he chuckled as he looked up at Mary and Suzie.

Suzie forced herself to look away from the bottle of beer. It was the same brand as the six pack that had been in Harry's refrigerator. The same beer that Jason had insisted his father would never drink. Now that she saw it in the mayor's hand things began to make sense to her. Perhaps the mayor had dropped by Dune House for a visit and had brought a six pack of his favorite beer. Maybe he insisted on Harry taking a few swigs with him. Harry, as fearful as he was of the man, probably would have complied. Could the poison have been in the beer?

But Suzie knew she was getting ahead of herself. She still had no idea why Thomas would want to kill Harry over a few photos. It was time to test the waters.

"Actually, we did have a harrowing incident the other day with the plumbing," Suzie began to describe finding something wedged in the drain of the sink. "Turns out, it was this," Suzie said as she fished the cufflink out of her purse and laid it on the table. Jason stared down at it, and then looked slowly up at her. Thomas barely skimmed his gaze over it.

"Oh, how strange," he shrugged and sipped his beer.

"Stranger still," Suzie said as she nudged the cufflink towards him. "It has your initials on it."

"Does it?" Thomas laughed. "I'm sure there are plenty of people with the initials TR."

"So, it's not yours?" Suzie asked and raised an eyebrow.

"Uh, well," Thomas picked up the cufflink and took a closer look at it. "Now that you mention it, this does look like a cufflink I've worn before. I must have lost it in Dune House years ago."

"Years ago?" Suzie asked and tilted her head slightly to the side. "So, you wouldn't have been wearing it recently?"

"I'm sorry, is there something unfashionable about cufflinks these days?" Thomas asked with a chuckle low in his throat. "I didn't realize that it was such an issue whether I wore them or not."

"Oh no, not at all," Suzie said quickly and flashed him an even, cool smile. "I just thought I'd search for the other one for you, if you'd lost them recently."

"Nope, it's been years," Thomas repeated with certainty. "I'm sure you wouldn't be able to find the other one even if you tried. I spent a lot of time at Dune House when Jason was a boy, didn't I, son?" he asked as he looked over at Jason.

"Yes, you did," Jason replied though his gaze was lingering on the cufflink. "Our families were close," Jason explained to Mary and Suzie. "My mother and Samantha were best friends," he added in a softer tone. "I still can't understand why Samantha ran off."

"Oh well, that's not dinner talk, Jason," Thomas said sharply. "We don't need to air our family business."

"I am family, too," Suzie spoke up with determination. "And I'd love to hear anything that Jason has to share."

"Sometimes I think about her," Jason admitted as he toyed with the cufflink. "I wonder where she's gone and what life she's living now. Don't you, Thomas?" he asked as he looked over at the man beside him.

"Jason, it's only been a few weeks. She'll run it out of her system, and I'm sure she'll be back in no time," Thomas sighed as if he carried the burdens of every person who roamed the earth. "Sometimes being married to a free spirit is hard."

"You poor thing," Mary replied with just enough edge to her words that Suzie could tell she meant it sarcastically. Luckily, before Jason or Thomas could pick up on it the waitress was back with their wines.

"I understand that you're part of the family, Suzie," Thomas said after the waitress walked away. "But this isn't just about the Allens. Garber is its own special kind of family. We all know each other, and have known each other for decades. We trust each other. Surely you can appreciate that," he smiled.

"I suppose," Suzie nodded and cast a smile in Mary's direction. "Mary is more like my sister than my friend, so I can understand that family is not just limited to blood."

"Exactly," Thomas smiled. "That's why I was surprised when Jason didn't inherit Dune House. I had hoped that you would be interested in following his wishes, since truly you should have no claim to the property."

"Well, from what I understand your only interest in the property is to flatten it," Suzie reminded Thomas and glanced over at Jason. "Isn't that right, Jason?" she asked. Jason nodded as if he was coming out of a daze.

"It's what's best for everyone," he insisted.

"Don't you have any fond memories of your home, Jason?" Suzie asked in a softer tone.

"Surely there are some experiences you treasure," Mary prompted him as well.

"Sometimes the darker memories outweigh even the most precious memories," Thomas interrupted in an attempt to change the subject. "Are you ladies ready to order?"

Jason was still staring wistfully at the cufflink.

"Actually, I am a little more tired than I

expected," Suzie said as she picked up the cufflink. "How about you, Mary?" she asked as she looked over at her friend.

"Me, too," Mary agreed. "Didn't know how tired I was until I sat down."

"I think we're going to call it a night," Suzie said with a slow smile as she looked back at Thomas. "But you two, enjoy your meal," she added as she stood up from the table. "And as for Dune House, my uncle left it to me, because he trusted me to value it and protect it. Obviously that trust you spoke of doesn't run through every home in Garber," she turned on her heel and walked away from the table with Mary right behind her. They had almost made it to the car when Jason caught up with them.

"What was all that about?" he asked sharply.

"Sorry, Jason, but I don't like that man," Suzie said as she turned to face him. "I don't trust him."

Jason frowned as he met her eyes, and then nodded a little. "Do you still have that cufflink?"

"Sure," Suzie opened her hand to reveal it.

"He said he lost it years ago, but I gave these to him," Jason said grimly. "I bought them for him right after my mother died, because he was so there for me. But I know for certain that I saw him wearing them about a month ago."

"Jason, we know for certain that he was wearing those cufflinks about three weeks ago," Suzie said and reached into the envelope in her purse. She pulled out the photographs from inside of it. "These are what your father left in the safety deposit box, Jason. I'm afraid that something might have happened to Samantha."

Jason's eyes widened as he sorted through the photos. "Are there more?" he asked in a grave tone.

"Not printed," Suzie replied. "I have this flash drive that I haven't looked into yet," she showed him the small drive. "Maybe there are more on here."

"Let me have it," Jason said, and extended his hand. Suzie looked at him with uncertainty. She was sure that the flash drive might have further proof of what really happened to Samantha, and in turn what might have really happened to her uncle. If she gave the flash drive to Jason there was a good chance that he would give it to Thomas.

"It's okay, Suzie," Mary said from beside her. "You can trust him."

Jason looked over at Mary with surprise, and then back to Suzie. "You can," he promised her. "I'll look at it at the police station."

"Call me the minute you find anything," Suzie requested as she pressed the flash drive into the palm of Jason's hand. "And please be careful, Jason. I know that you value Thomas' friendship, but if what I suspect about him is true, he's never been a friend to you."

"I will be," Jason promised her as he tucked the flash drive into his pocket. When he walked back towards the restaurant Suzie wondered if she had made a terrible mistake.

"How did you know that I could trust him?" she asked Mary as they walked to the car.

"It's in his eyes," Mary explained and smiled faintly. "I always knew when my kids were lying. They would get a little shine in their eyes. There wasn't any shine in his, just hurt. He needs to know the truth about Thomas, and about his father. If that flash drive helps him to find it, then no matter what comes of all of this, we will have had a good reason to be here."

Suzie nodded and unlocked the car doors. The entire drive home however, she couldn't stop thinking about that beer that had been left in the fridge.

Chapter Eight

Early the next morning when Suzie woke up she found Mary was already awake and making coffee.

"Mary, they didn't haul off all of that garbage yet, did they?" Suzie asked.

"No, it's still in a pile on the side of the house," Mary replied as she fixed their coffee. "Why?" when she turned around with the two mugs of coffee she found that Suzie was gone. Suzie was digging through the garbage bags. She could recall carefully placing the glass bottles she had found in the living room into the trash bags to make sure they didn't break. She found them fairly easily.

"What are you doing?" Mary asked with growing concern.

"This is what I think happened, Mary," Suzie explained as she held up the beer bottles. "I think that Harry saw Thomas and Samantha walk down to the water. I think he took photos of what he thought was going to be a romantic evening. I think he took photos of them arguing, and then much more than that. I think Thomas killed Samantha because she threatened to leave him and expose him, and I think Harry saw it all," she frowned as she carried the bottles back into the house.

"I think that when Harry took the photographs to be printed as proof, the clerk in the store spotted what was on the photographs and alerted Thomas, that's why all of the photos weren't printed. Before Harry had a chance to print them again, Thomas stopped by with some beer. At this point, after witnessing such a horrific crime, I think Harry was terrified of the man. So, when Thomas insisted on him drinking one of the beers, he probably did. He had no idea that the beer was poisoned. That's why Thomas was so bent on having this place bulldozed. He wanted to make sure that any evidence was turned into rubble," she shook her head as she wrapped the bottles in plastic bags. "But I bet Dr. Rose can pull something out of these bottles that will show just what poison was used."

"You should take them to the station," Mary insisted. "I would go with you, but I have to wait for Kent to fax me some paperwork. I managed to hook up the computer and the internet so I could receive it and print it. If I don't get it back to him today this is going to drag on forever."

"It's fine, it's better if you stay here where it's safe," Suzie said sternly. "Don't leave the house unless you text me. Until we get all of this figured out we could be at risk."

"I'll be careful," Mary promised. "You be careful, too."

"I will be," Suzie hugged her friend tightly then hurried to the car. She wanted to get to the station and find out if Jason had found anything on the flash drive.

***

When Suzie walked into the station she found Jason leaning over a man's shoulder at a computer.

"Hi Suzie," Jason said as he straightened up. "Sorry, but we didn't find anything yet. Looks like the drive was wiped clean somehow. What's that you have there?" he asked curiously as he looked at the plastic bags.

"Just something for Dr. Rose," Suzie explained.

"She's out for the moment, she'll be in by ten though. This is Carter, our IT tech," he added as he patted the man's shoulder. Carter was too busy staring at the screen to greet her.

"Oh yes," Carter muttered as he scrolled through the computer screen. "I found it," he snapped his fingers and laughed shortly.

"Found what?" Suzie asked as she leaned over his shoulder.

Jason rested his hands on the desk on the other side of Carter and leaned in closely as well. "What is it?" he asked in a more gruff tone.

"Well, you see people think when they delete things, that they just disappear, but that's not the case. A copy of whatever they have deleted usually remains, as is the case here," he added as he clicked the mouse. When he did, photographs began to populate the screen.

"Oh no," Suzie gasped as she saw the images

121

before her. "Thomas was with his wife that night on the beach, but not for a romantic evening," she shook her head. The images revealed that Thomas had actually struck his wife very hard over the head with the bottle of wine he had been carrying. Then he let her body be washed away by the sea. Suzie thought of her uncle taking those photos. "Uncle Harry must have been horrified," she murmured.

"He knew there wasn't time," Jason said quietly as he stared at the screen. "He knew there wasn't time to get down there to help her, so he made sure he had evidence instead. All this time," he growled as he stood up straight. "I trusted that man more than my own father!"

"Jason, it's not your fault he fooled you," Suzie tried to calm him as she met his eyes. "You were hurting, and you needed someone, there's no shame in that."

"There is if the man I turned to is also my father's murderer," Jason countered as he snatched up his hat and began walking towards the front of the police station.

"Jason, where are you going?" Suzie called

out with concern.

"I'm going to arrest the mayor," he replied sharply. Suzie ran to catch up with him and made it to his side just in time as he reached his patrol car.

"Jason wait, don't you think it would be better to send someone else?" Suzie pleaded. "What if he knows that you know?"

"I'll be fine, Suzie," he assured her and started the engine of the car. "I wouldn't let anyone else put the handcuffs on that man."

As Suzie watched Jason drive away she felt a subtle sense of relief despite the chaos of the last few minutes. She was glad that Jason finally knew that his father had been trying to be a better man than he had been in the past. He had stuck his neck out in an attempt to right a wrong, unfortunately he had suffered for his attempt. She only hoped that Jason wouldn't put himself in a similar position. Suzie was still thinking about this when she pulled into the driveway at Dune House. She walked up onto the porch and called out as she walked in the door.

"Mary, I'm here, sorry it took me longer than

I expected..." she was suddenly silenced by the presence of Thomas standing beside the fireplace. Her purse slipped off her arm and fell to the floor.

"So glad you could join us, Suzie," he said and gestured to the chair across from the fireplace. Suzie noticed Mary sitting in the opposite chair, her eyes wide, and her lips drawn tight with fear.

"What are you doing here?" Suzie asked with growing animosity.

"Oh, can't I just drop by for a visit?" Thomas asked with a shrug. "I just wanted to see the progress you two have made. I must say it's pretty amazing. It's a shame no one else is going to see it," he added as he used the poker he held in his hand to stir the ashes in the fireplace.

"What are you talking about?" Suzie demanded. She hoped he didn't know what they had discovered.

"You know, I thought to myself, these two ladies they're not going to find anything. They'll lose interest and move on. So, imagine my surprise when I discovered that you had been doing a little investigating, Suzie?" he laughed a little and shook his head. "The thing about small towns, is that you can't keep secrets. Especially from the mayor. I own just about every person in this town, and I will do anything it takes to make sure that my secrets are kept. Yours however, are public knowledge," he stirred the ashes again. "Sit down, Suzie."

"I'll stand," Suzie replied and stood beside Mary's chair. "I want to know what all this is about."

"I know you went to the bank, I know that you took those photos to the library, I know that you had Carter analyzing something at the police station. I know," he said in a cruel tone as he stepped closer to her, "that Jason is on his way to arrest me. Can you imagine that? Me? I've been nothing but caring to that boy, and this is how he repays me."

"I wouldn't call killing his father caring," Suzie replied through gritted teeth. She held his gaze steadily. She was determined not to let him see how terrified she was.

"Try proving it," Thomas suggested with a

chuckle. "Good ol' Harry died of a broken heart. Isn't that poetic enough for you?" he asked. "The old man could have passed away in here and rotted for years without anyone noticing, least of all his son. So really, was it so tragic for me to take a life that was being wasted?"

"You're a terrible person," Suzie said flatly as she crossed her arms. "You're so smug, thinking that you got away with two murders. But you haven't got away with anything."

"Two?" Thomas narrowed his eyes sharply and took a step closer to her. "By the time I'm done here, honey, it's going to be four."

With that he picked up some rope that was laying in a pile behind him.

"Mary, come on, we have to get out of here," Suzie said in a hiss and reached for her friend's hand. Only then did she realize that Mary was tied to the chair by her ankles.

"What are you doing?" she asked with horror as she turned back to Thomas to find he was trailing gasoline in a circle around the two chairs. When he put the gas can down, he pulled out a gun he had tucked in the back of his pants.

Suzie's heart was racing. He pointed the gun at Mary.

"Get in the chair, or I do this now," he said sharply. Suzie knew that the moment she was tied up in the chair there would be no hope of either of them escaping, but she couldn't leave Mary alone.

"Don't do this, Thomas, think of your career," Suzie spoke quickly. "Think of spending your life behind bars!"

"I don't need to think about either," he barked back. "I did what I had to do. Samantha was going to leave me. She was going to tell the world about my illegal dealings. How would it make me look to have my own wife saying these things about me? What do you think that would do to a wholesome image like mine? If your uncle had just stayed out of it, then none of this would have happened," he pointed out. "But he didn't, so now, it has to happen. Sit down," he commanded her sternly.

Suzie reluctantly sat down in the high backed chair. She grabbed onto Mary's hand as Thomas wrapped the rope around their wrists and around Suzie's ankles.

"Look on the bright side, ladies, at least you won't be going alone. And, in the future this will be the sight of a resort," he smiled up at them. Suzie was startled by how ruthless he was. She knew no amount of pleading would stop him. She tried to think of a way to escape, but with her heart racing and her mind spinning, she couldn't think of a single thing.

"Please, we won't say anything to anyone," Mary promised as she squeezed Suzie's hand.

"If only I could believe that," he sighed and pulled a pack of matches out of his pocket.

"Stop!" Jason shouted from the door that Suzie had left open. He had his gun drawn and was aiming it straight at Thomas. "Drop the matches," Jason demanded.

"Sure, just let me light them first," Thomas chuckled and began fumbling with them.

"Don't do it, I will shoot you," Jason warned him as he stepped closer.

"You're not going to shoot me, Jason," Thomas rolled his eyes. "Are you forgetting that

I've seen you bawl your eyes out over your poor father? I know you, kid, you're not going to shoot..."

The sound of the gun being fired was so deafening that at first Suzie thought it was an explosion. She looked up in horror, expecting to see Thomas slumped over on the floor. Instead she saw him cowering close to the fireplace. He had dropped the matches. The bullet Jason fired was lodged into the wall just above where Thomas' shoulder had been.

"You're under arrest," Jason declared as he moved closer to him.

Outside Dune House sirens and tires squealed as patrol cars arrived to back up Jason. Other officers rushed in to handcuff Thomas, but Jason stopped them.

"I want to do it," he said firmly. Once the mayor was in custody and had been taken out of the house, Jason walked over to Suzie and Mary who had stepped outside onto the porch.

"How did you know that he'd be here?" Suzie asked as she and Mary gulped down the fresh air that came from the sea. Having been so close to being killed was enough reason to savor every breath.

"I was driving over there, when I remembered that Thomas paid for all three of the desk sergeant's kids to go through college. It seemed generous at the time, but the more I thought about it, and what we'd learned about Thomas, the more I wondered if it was a way to get information out of the police station. Then I thought about what Thomas would do if he knew that you two had found those photographs. Of course, after finding out about him killing his wife I knew what he was capable of, so I thought it best that I come back and check on you," he sighed and shook his head. "I'm so glad I did."

"So are we," Mary laughed, her hands still shaking with fear. "When he burst in, I didn't know what to think. I just pretended I didn't know anything. I didn't know what else to do. Then he pulled the gun on me, and," she sighed. "I've never been so afraid."

"I'm sorry, Mary," Suzie hugged her tightly. "I had no idea it would turn out like this. I need to get you home."

"Home?" Mary asked with a faint smile. "I don't have a home to go back to, remember? Yes, I was scared, but Suzie you were there, and then Jason came. It was actually rather thrilling," she admitted in a sheepish tone.

"Do you think he has any chance of going free?" Suzie asked as she looked back at Jason.

"Not with the photos we have, and what Dr. Rose will likely find in those beer bottles, and now this," he added as he frowned in the direction of the ropes hanging off the chairs. "Thomas has always had a strong influence on the people of this town, but never once did I think he was a criminal. I guess I trusted him too easily," he blinked a few times then wiped at his eyes. "I need to get back to the station, are you two okay or would you like to be checked out at the hospital?"

"We're fine," Mary said quickly.

"Yes, thanks to you," Suzie added. "But wait just a moment, Jason," she requested as she walked over to her purse which she had dropped on the floor. She pulled out the envelope that she had found in some of Harry's things. "I think it's time you read this," she said softly and pressed it into his hand. He stared at her with a puzzled look. "Give your father a chance, Jason, grief can cause people to behave in the strangest ways. I might not have known your father well, but since I've been here I've learned a thing or two about him. I've learned that he was willing to risk his own life to reveal the truth, and I've learned that he loved you more than he was ever brave enough to say."

"I'll read it," Jason promised with a slow nod. As he walked out through the door of Dune House, Suzie felt a strange sense of relief. She almost felt as if her Uncle Harry was walking out right along with him.

***

By the time the stars rose that evening, Suzie was exhausted again. But it was a nice feeling. She and Mary had straightened out the living room after forensics had done a sweep of it. They left behind more dust of course. There was still a lot to do to get the B & B ready to open, but together Suzie had no doubt that they could do it.

Suzie had invited Jason over to join them for a glass of wine on the porch after such a long and adrenaline-filled day. She wasn't sure if he would take her up on it, but she hoped he would. When she settled down on the chair beside Mary she felt at peace for the first time in a long time. With her best friend beside her, and the ocean stretched out before her, she felt as if there were no longer any limitations to the possibilities in her life. Stranger still, when she watched the rolling waves, she thought of Paul for the first time since he had caught her mid-fall at the motel. She wondered whether he was still on solid ground, or if he was back out on the waves.

"Last week I never would have thought of us being here," Mary chuckled to herself as she too looked out over the water. "It's amazing the turns life takes."

When they heard the squeak of the door to the porch they both looked up to find Jason walking out onto the porch with his own glass of wine. He settled into a chair beside Suzie and sipped at his glass.

"I have to admit, Suzie, when you came into town, I never imagined that you would change my life this much," he glanced over at her with a smile. She could see the lightness in his eyes, and his more relaxed nature. She was sure that he had read the letter. She hoped it meant as much to him as it had meant to her to read it. Though she had never known her uncle very well, she was glad that he thought he could trust her, for whatever reason, and that together with Mary's help, and Jason's instincts, she had been able to solve the mystery of not just Harry's death, but Samantha's as well.

"To be honest, I never imagined that my life would change this much," Suzie laughed.

"Me neither," Mary agreed.

"So, have you two decided are you selling or staying?" Jason asked as he looked between them.

"Staying," Suzie and Mary said at the same time, and then laughed at one another. "The plan is to finish refurbishing the house and then to see how we go running it as a B & B. We both wanted some excitement in our lives," Suzie explained to Jason who was grinning.

"And we sure did find it here," Mary added as she took a sip of her wine. The waves rushed to the shore, crashing, only to retreat again. The sounds and scents that filled the air had a soothing quality that coaxed all three of them into a shared silence of appreciation. Dune House was alive again. What other secrets might its walls hold?

The End

***

The next book in the Dune House Cozy Mystery Series, 'Boats and Bad Guys' is available now.

From the Author

Thank you very much for reading Seaside Secrets, the first book in the Dune House Cozy Mystery series.

You might like the first book in my Chocolate Centered Cozy Mystery Series, The Sweet Smell of Murder. I have included an excerpt at the end of the book

If you enjoyed the book and would like to be updated when I release a new book you can sign up for email updates at http://www.cindybellbooks.com/newsletter. I will never share your email and you will only receive emails from me when I have released a new book, am offering a discount or when I have giveaways.

More Cozy Mysteries by Cindy Bell

Dune House Cozy Mysteries

Seaside Secrets

Boats and Bad Guys

Treasured History

Hidden Hideaways

Dodgy Dealings

Suspects and Surprises

Sage Gardens Cozy Mysteries

Birthdays Can Be Deadly

Money Can Be Deadly

Trust Can Be Deadly

Ties Can Be Deadly

Chocolate Centered Cozy Mysteries

The Sweet Smell of Murder

Heavenly Highland Inn Cozy Mysteries

Murdering the Roses

Dead in the Daisies

Killing the Carnations

Drowning the Daffodils

Suffocating the Sunflowers

Books, Bullets and Blooms

A Deadly serious Gardening Contest

A Bridal Bouquet and a Body

Wendy the Wedding Planner Cozy Mysteries

Matrimony, Money and Murder

Chefs, Ceremonies and Crimes

Knives and Nuptials

Mice, Marriage and Murder

Excerpt from *The Sweet Smell of Murder*

Screeching tires jolted Ally Sweet from the relaxed state she had settled into. A car swerved across the highway in front of hers. It corrected, and straightened out into the lane. A quick shake of her head cleared the panic caused by the near-collision.

"Peaches, you okay?" She looked over at the carrier buckled into the passenger seat beside her. After receiving a reassuring meow Ally focused on the traffic around her. It was a familiar drive, but over the years it had become much more congested. She was relieved when she finally passed the city limits sign.

Ally grew up an hour outside of the city, but her hometown was like another planet. She was just taking a short break, but her heart ached as she knew she was finally leaving behind not just a broken marriage, but also the life she had built.

However, the draw of where she was headed kept her tears at bay. Going home triggered memories of heat billowing out of an oven door, or laughter filtering in from the back porch, of little fingers plucking at piano keys.

Ally longed for the presence of her grandmother in ways that she longed for little else. She seemed to make the world make sense, and if it didn't for some reason, she would put it back in place. Ally took the next exit off the highway. The sign boasted 'Mainbry', but the name of the small town where she was headed was Blue River. The town got its name from the glistening blue river running through it. After only a few miles the scenery changed from pavement and concrete to fields dotted with cows and a handful of farm houses. A whiff of manure, freshly cut grass, and the promise of rain, was the smell that greeted Ally. She was home.

She turned down the long, dirt driveway of her grandmother's property with a sense of completion bolstering her. Whenever she heard the crunch of the rough road beneath the tires of her car she knew that she was home. She only had one foot out of the car when the front door of the small cottage burst open.

"Ally! Ally! Oh she's here, Arnold!" A petite, gray-haired woman wearing a bright floral dress bounded down the steps of the front porch. On her lightly lipsticked mouth was the biggest grin that Ally had ever seen. She always thought her grandmother had a way of sharing how she was feeling without ever saying a word. Without hesitation she rushed forward to meet her grandmother at the bottom of the steps. Her initials were carved into one corner of the bottom step. A fond smile rose to her lips at the memory of etching them into the soft wood. She opened her arms to her grandmother as she had ever since she was a little girl. Arnold charged right up beside her.

"Hi Mee-Maw, hi Arnold." Ally's heart swelled with love at the sensation of her grandmother's arms wrapping around her. She didn't even mind that Arnold was sniffing at her pocket. Arnold was known around town for his good sniffer.

"Arnold, do be polite." Charlotte clucked her tongue with disapproval. Arnold scurried off into the house. For a rather portly pot-bellied pig he could actually move pretty fast.

"Let me look at you, honey." Charlotte swept her piercing gaze over Ally from the top of her head to the tips of her toes. Ally didn't feel criticized. Her grandmother had been looking her over this way since she was a young child. "My my, the city did good things for you."

"Did it?" Ally looked at her with a sullen frown. "Doesn't really feel that way."

"Well, you just need some sun on your cheeks and some chocolate in your belly." She laughed and waved Ally into the house. Ally followed after her. There was little in life that she loved more than spending time with her grandmother. Their relationship had blossomed from parent and child to a close friendship.

The inside of the cottage was just as she remembered it. There were soft reminders of the past everywhere in picture frames, needlepoint, and even old pictures that Ally had painted as a child. She shouldn't have been surprised as it hadn't been that long since she had been there last, but after everything that had happened over the past few months she felt as if it had been a century.

"Come, have some tea with me." Charlotte steered her into the kitchen. The kitchen held the most intense memories for Ally. She had spent hours as a young child sitting underneath the round kitchen table. She would play with her dolls, or imagine new worlds, while the grown-ups above her discussed all of the heavy things that life had dealt. Ally was under that table the day her mother admitted that Ally's father had simply walked away. Ally barely remembered the exact words, but she did remember the scent of vanilla and cinnamon, which her grandmother always put in her tea.

"Here you are." Charlotte set down Ally's favorite cup and saucer. It was a sky blue set with big yellow stars painted on the side. Ally's mother had made it when she was a child. Ally picked up the cup as she sat down.

"Thanks, Mee-Maw."

"I've missed you."

"I've missed you, too." Ally looked into her eyes. "More than you know."

"What's going on, my love?" Charlotte reached across the table and took Ally's free hand in her own. "Tell me all about it."

"I just wanted to come for a visit."

Peaches rubbed her long, orange body along Ally's leg. She felt the tickle of the cat's tail.

"I'm sure you did. But I'm sure there's a lot more to it than that. Hmm?" She arched a perfectly sculpted eyebrow. Ally always admired her grandmother's beauty. It was classic in the sense that it didn't require a lot of make-up. Her features were more strong than feminine, and her flowing, gray hair should have aged her. Instead, to Ally, it made her grandmother magical. The bold green eyes that gazed at her were the same that Ally saw in the mirror each day. They weren't just a similar shade, they were the same shape and color. When Ally looked into her grandmother's eyes, she found it very difficult to tell a lie. This little problem had made getting through high school challenging for her.

"All right, all right." Ally sighed and took a sip of her tea. As she set the saucer back down she rounded her shoulders forward. "I might not be handling the divorce as well as I first thought."

"Well, how does one handle something like that?" Charlotte's lips pursed briefly as if she was trying to hold back a tirade. This was fairly unusual for her, as Ally was used to her grandmother always saying what she thought. "I mean, it's not as if you changed dentists, we're talking about the breaking of vows."

"It wasn't like that, Mee-Maw. We just didn't

get along anymore."

"Because he's a heartless, immature beast of a man who wants nothing more than a servant for a wife." Charlotte smacked the table lightly with her fingertips. "Does that about cover it?"

Ally tried not to smile. "Mee-Maw, there's two sides to every story. I was at fault, too. It just didn't work out."

"So, do you think he's sipping tea and thinking about it somewhere?"

Ally's cheeks flushed. She knew that he wasn't. In fact she was fairly certain that he was with a friend of hers, and not likely thinking about her at all.

"No, I guess not."

"See?" Charlotte shook her head. "Honey, I've always told you, you've got a big heart, and that's beautiful, but your brain has got to be bigger."

"Mee-maw!"

"I'm sorry. I'm just telling the truth."

Charlotte blushed a little. "Was that too far?"

"I just thought it would get better. I mean, everyone kept telling me, just give it a few more years, it will get better." Ally took the last sip of her tea, with the hope that it would calm her nerves.

"I never told you that."

"You're right. You were the only one that didn't." Ally stared down at the table top. Her mind flooded with the memories of all of the conversations she and her grandmother had shared regarding her marriage. Not once did her grandmother advise her to wait it out. Instead she had pointed out that Ally had already given up so much of herself, and still he was not content. Ally's eyes moistened with tears.

"Hey now, beautiful." Charlotte caught Ally by the chin and tilted her head up so that she could meet her eyes. "You didn't do anything wrong. Love is love, and it will do as it pleases. Unfortunately, you are not the first woman in this family to marry the wrong man, and I feel certain you won't be the last."

"Is that supposed to make me feel better, Mee-Maw?" Ally offered a half-smile. She blinked back her tears.

"There's nothing I can say to make you feel better. That's entirely up to you." She gave Ally's chin a light pinch. "Don't you fret though. There are millions of men on this earth."

"Oh no, thank you, I gave it a go, I think I'll fly solo from now on." Ally stood up to clear away the tea cups from the table.

"We'll see, we'll see. One thing is for sure, we need to get you into the shop. That will help clear your head."

"I am really looking forward to that." Ally smiled as she thought of all of the time she had spent in her grandmother's handmade, gourmet chocolate and coffee shop as a child. The quaint shop served as a place to disappear from the world, and let go of all of her troubles, past and present. She had loved working with her grandmother in the shop and when she had first graduated from college she took a chocolatier's course with the hopes of opening her own chocolate shop. But soon after completing the course she met her husband and her well laid plans were put on hold.

"Good, because there's plenty to do. My gift basket business has really taken off." She paused a moment and met Ally's eyes. "I could really use the help."

Ally drew a breath in surprise at her grandmother's clear request. Although Blue River was a small country town, Charlotte's handmade chocolates had been very popular for years and were in increasing demand. Charlotte had started the shop as a coffee shop, gradually she began experimenting with making chocolates and what started off as a hobby soon blossomed into a flourishing passion and business. "Why didn't you tell me? I would have come to visit sooner."

"Because I don't just want you to come to visit, Ally. I want you to come to stay." Charlotte shook her head. "I'm getting older, darling, I need to rest."

"Don't even talk like that, Mee-Maw!" Ally narrowed her eyes. A wave of dread consumed her. The very thought of her grandmother reaching an age where she felt less capable left her heart fluttering.

"Calm down, calm down, it's not like I'm going to kick it tomorrow." Charlotte laughed. "I'm just saying it would be nice to have the help. Business is growing and you can help expand it further."

Ally stared at her with parted lips and widened eyes. She wasn't quite sure how to process what her grandmother was saying. "You want me to move back here?"

"Would that be so terrible?" Her grandmother looked into her eyes. "You were happy here once."

"I was just a kid. Of course I was happy here," Ally said. "I don't know. I mean, of course I want to help, but I do have a life in the city, my job..."

"Which you hate." Charlotte raised an eyebrow.

"Well, I don't hate it but it's a bit boring." Ally frowned.

"A bit?" Charlotte grinned. "I know that you feel like you're wasting your time there. Life is about passion, not the numbers on a paycheck. Listen Ally, I'm not asking you to stay now. I just want you to think about what you want in the future. I had always assumed, well hoped, you would take over the shop, but if that's not something you want, that's okay. It's your life, sweetie, and you've got to live it the way you choose. I'm thinking about my future, too, and I need to know if I need to think about someone else taking over the shop."

"I do want to take over the shop, absolutely. I just hate the idea of you not running it." Ally's mind spun with all of the thoughts that hadn't even been on her mind when she first arrived in town. It was difficult to think of her grandmother getting older. Ally felt as if she was the type of woman that was too strong and fierce to ever truly age. "Let me think about it, okay?"

"Sure." She gave Ally's hand a squeeze. "Just remember you don't have to do anything anybody else wants you to do. You don't have to be anybody but who you are. That oaf of an ex-husband had your head turned around. Now it's time to think about what you really want."

Ally squeezed her grandmother's hand in return. She smiled warmly at her. Her grandmother's words could be harsh, but they were always true. Daniel had insisted that she give up her dream of being a chocolatier and go to college, that she get her masters in business. It was all part of their five year plan before having children. He was determined that they would be wealthy. Ally understood the logic, but it did go against her values to some degree. Still, she had fully committed to their plan. What wasn't part of that plan was Daniel's roaming eye and his neglect, and most importantly the fact that they were never ever really suited for each other. She grimaced as she recalled the final arguments they went through.

"Thanks, Mee-Maw, I needed to hear that."

Charlotte gave her a kind smile. "It hurts, baby, don't let anyone tell you it doesn't. But it does get easier. It gets easier a lot faster when you let someone new into your life."

"No, absolutely not, no way, Mee-Maw. I'm not interested." Ally looked at her with a stern frown. "You know I love you, and I respect you, but please do not get in the middle of my romantic life."

"Would I ever even consider it?" Charlotte's mouth formed into an innocent circle and she fluttered her hand at her chest. "Really Ally. What would make you worry about that?"

Ally arched her eyebrow. "Maybe prom?"

"Well, that was different."

"Not at all." Ally crossed her arms and fixed her grandmother with a stubborn glare.

"Very different. Brent was who you should have gone with. I just helped him out."

"Mee-Maw, I mean it." Ally set her cup of tea down and yawned. "I'm a little worn out from the drive."

"You take a rest. I'm going to take Arnold for a walk."

Ally tried not to giggle. Her grandmother always took Arnold for walks. Most of the neighbors were used to it, but some still gawked. Yes, they lived in the country, but Charlotte was the only one who had a pot-belly pig for a pet. Ally gave her grandmother a quick hug. Then she headed for her room. The cottage was only two bedrooms. One had been Ally's for as long as she could remember. It was painted a strange shade of purple that she had picked out when she was six. It was a gorgeous color to her then. Now Ally wasn't sure what to call it. Her bed was just as she had left it, with a thick quilt sewn by her great-grandmother spread across it.

Charlotte embraced tradition in their family,

from heirlooms to etiquette. However, she was not too strict when it came to the choices that Ally made. The walls of Ally's room were still hung with clippings and memorabilia from her high school years. As Ally sat down on the foot of her bed, Peaches jumped up beside her. Ally stroked the cat's fur. Her eyes swept around the room. In many ways it felt like a time capsule. She remembered spending hours dreaming about what it would be like to run away to the city. She thought her dreams would come true there. She never imagined that one day she would be curled up in her king-sized bed in her luxury apartment weeping for the simplicity of her childhood.

Ally sighed and walked over to the dresser. She still stored her country clothes in it. While living in the city she had acquired a more refined taste, only because she felt as if she embarrassed Daniel in her denim and flannel. She began to realize that her grandmother was right. She had changed so much of herself to please Daniel.

Maybe being back home for a while would give her the opportunity to find herself again. She changed into some comfortable clothes and then settled back in her bed. She stretched out. Immediately she was assaulted by tiny paws and a fluffy head. Peaches bumped her head against Ally's chin and rubbed her cheek across Ally's. Ally smiled and nuzzled her right back. One good thing had come out of the city, her best feline friend.

"I know you're glad to be here, too. Lots of fat rats to chase." She scratched lightly at the top of the cat's head. Peaches purred. She flicked her tail with delight. "I guess we'll just have to see how we both like it here. Maybe it is time for a change."

As she laid back and closed her eyes, Ally felt a tug on her heart. Her childhood home held a lot of beautiful memories, but it also held a lot of painful ones. In particular the memory of her mother's battle with illness. She and Ally had moved back in with Charlotte as she went through treatment. Ally had been too young to really understand, but she had felt the tension and sorrow in the home. Charlotte had transformed all of that by making their last days together one of celebration and joy. Ally still felt that subtle ache though. Her grandmother had been there for her every single day of her life since her mother passed, which kept Ally from feeling too lost, but she did wish her mother had been there as well.

As she struggled to clear her mind and fall asleep Ally felt the comfort of her great-grandmother's quilt over her, and the warmth and love contained in the walls of the cottage washed over her. She might not be able to decide if she was going to move back or not, but in that moment she knew that she was exactly where she needed to be.

The Sweet Smell of Murder is available now.

Made in United States
Troutdale, OR
11/12/2024

24725833R00096